FOLLOW ME

FOLLOW ME

K. R. Alexander

Scholastic Inc.

The publisher does not have any control over and does not assume any responsibility for author or third-party websites or their content.

No part of this publication may be reproduced, stored in a retrieval system, or transmitted in any form or by any means, electronic, mechanical, photocopying, recording, or otherwise, without written permission of the publisher. For information regarding permission, write to Scholastic Inc., Attention: Permissions Department, 557 Broadway, New York, NY 10012.

This book is a work of fiction. Names, characters, places, and incidents are either the product of the author's imagination or are used fictitiously, and any resemblance to actual persons, living or dead, business establishments, events, or locales is entirely coincidental.

ISBN 978-1-338-33888-1

10 9 8 7 6 5 4 3 2 1   20 21 22 23 24

Printed in the U.S.A.   40
First printing 2020

Book design by Baily Crawford

I see her at the corners of my vision.

The ghost of the girl, carrying an old teddy bear.

I see her, but I don't see her eyes. Don't see her face. Just the black hair obscuring pale white skin.

I know what will happen when I see her face. I know because it's happened before—my new friends told me.

They tell me I need to get out of here immediately, before it's too late.

Because the girl is getting closer.

Every time I see her.

In the mirror.

In the hallway.

Outside my door.

Closer by an inch every time.

Every time, only an inch.

But those inches add up.

My friends are wrong, though.

Moving won't help.

She's following me. Everywhere I go. There's no escape.

It's already too late.

And when she reaches me, I'll never be seen again.

1

"I'm getting closer," she says, her voice echoing around the room. "I'm going to find you, Tamal. I'm going to get you!"

I squeeze my head to my knees because if I can't see her, she can't see me, and I'm already as hidden as I can be up here, tucked away behind the moving boxes and covered with a blanket that had—only moments ago—been wrapped around my great-grandmother's old rocking chair. It's the perfect hiding place. But I can't convince myself it's good enough to avoid her.

The floorboards creak.

Inches away from my hiding place.

I don't peek.

I know if I do I'll see her feet under the gap in the blanket.

I know if I do, she'll find me.

I try not to breathe. Try not to move the slightest bit.

The floor creaks again.

She's moving away.

I let out a sigh.

"Gotcha!" she yells, tossing the blanket off me.

"Aww," I moan. I collapse back on the carpet and look up at my new friend Lela. Even though my family just moved here, we're already fast friends. It helps that she was the first person I spoke to my first day of fourth grade. It also helps that she really wanted to check out my house.

She giggles at my look of defeat. "That's no fair," I say. "I totally saw you peeking when I went to hide."

"Did not!" she says. Her hands go to her hips. "You're just angry that I found you first. I still have to find Max. Did you see which way he went?"

I open my mouth to tell her that he isn't up here—I saw him going toward the kitchen when we ran off to hide—but catch myself. Her smile widens.

"Nice try," I say.

"Not even a little hint? This place is *massive*."

She's telling me.

We've been in our new house a whole week, and I still haven't memorized the layout. There are at least a dozen bedrooms and as many bathrooms, and there are three whole stories to explore. Not including the basement—not that I'd ever go down there unless Mom made me go do the laundry. The mansion is monstrously large, but somehow costs the same as our two-bedroom condo in New York. I guess moving to the country has its perks. We get to stay in a sprawling mansion.

"Fine," she says when I shake my head. "I'll find him myself, then. He's a lot better at hiding, though, so it might take a while. You have to stay here and . . . unpack as punishment!"

She winks, then turns on her heel and runs off down the hall.

I try not to take her remark personally. I mean, I barely know her or Max—I just met her at school on Monday—so I'm still getting used to her brand of humor. It's November, which means they've already been in school awhile. I'd honestly been terrified that I wouldn't make any friends, but the moment I showed up in class, Lela walked right over to me, Max beside her, and introduced the two of them.

"You must be the kid who moved into the manor house," she'd said. "Welcome."

And really, they were the only kids who *were* welcoming. Pretty much everyone else in class ignored me. I didn't know if it was because of the color of my skin or the fact that we'd moved into the biggest house in town, but it was unsettling. Lela and Max, though, didn't seem to care about any of that. We played together and swapped stories all through recess, and after school that first night, we went to the park until dark. Max's mom even drove me home, which was super kind, since my house is at the top of the hill and surrounded by woods.

Lela and Max had come with, and the moment we reached the house, Lela gasped in awe.

"Wow," she whispered, then looked at me. "I bet it's even cooler on the inside!"

Which, I guess, seemed like more than enough reason to invite the both of them here for game night.

Truth be told, I think they're both just excited to get to explore the house. Apparently, it's sort of a mystery to the kids in town. I'm just grateful for the company—we've barely been here a week, and the massive empty hallways and enormous rooms feel incredibly lonely, no matter how loudly my parents blare their music.

I stand by the door, listening to her run from room to room, calling out Max's name. It makes me smile. Even though we just met, I can tell that the three of us will be best friends. Which is good, because my parents were terrified that I'd have a hard time adjusting out here. If I ignore the strange looks I get from some of the other classmates, I'd say I'm doing a good job.

I think I'm having an easier time adjusting out here than I did back in NYC.

There, I didn't really have any friends. I didn't play sports, and I wasn't cool or smart enough to be in any of the clubs, and my school didn't have a band program until fifth grade, so I couldn't even play an instrument. Which just meant I spent a lot of recesses on my own. And weekends.

Hearing Lela wandering down the hall, singing

out "Oh, Maaa-aaax" as she searches for him, makes me smile. But then I remember that I'm supposed to be unpacking, as punishment for her finding me first, so I head back into the room and peel the tape from one of the boxes. Nothing but dishes inside. Ugh. This was supposed to be down in the kitchen. Two floors down.

I pick up the box when I feel it.

A tingling on the back of my neck. A cold breath. Someone watching me.

"He's not in here," I say to Lela. "I already told you."

I glance up.

Toward the standing mirror propped in the corner.

I can see all the way to the end of the hall.

To where a girl stands, clutching a teddy bear.

At first, I think it's Lela. That she found an old stuffed animal in one of my boxes and brought it out to mock me. But that isn't right. Lela's skin is dark and her hair is short and curly, and this girl is pale as a sheet, with long black hair. And that teddy bear is way too old to be mine.

More chills race down my arms.

Is the girl . . .

floating?

I drop the box and turn around.

The hall is empty. Completely empty.

Of course it's empty—it's just my friends and me here. My parents are out getting groceries for dinner. I furrow my eyebrows. Look back to the mirror. But it's just my reflection staring back. No girl at the end of the hall. Had she even been there in the first place?

I lean in closer, peering at myself in the mirror, and pull down my eyelids like that might reveal something. I just look tired. I look in closer, examining the whites of my eyes . . .

"What in the world are you doing?"

I jolt upright and turn around. Lela is standing there, Max looking crestfallen at her side.

"Found him," she says. "Now it's your turn. But be warned, I'm really, really good at this game."

She turns to go, but Max must notice I'm still sort of in shock.

"Are you okay?" he asks. He's a bit shorter than Lela, with short black ringlets of hair and wide shoulders—he's already playing football on the school team, but he's admitted he'd rather be playing trading card games than running laps.

I shrug. Look over their shoulders. There's no one at the end of the hall.

There never was, Tamal. There never was.

But I *know* I saw something. Some*one*. That was impossible, though, wasn't it?

Unless what my other classmates whispered was true.

Unless this place was really haunted.

"Yeah," I say. I put on my most convincing smile—trying to convince both them and myself that I wasn't seeing ghosts. "Just fine. Let's go."

We head down to the kitchen together to start the next round.

I swear I feel eyes on the back of my neck the entire way.

I don't look behind me.

I don't want to know what's waiting there.

3

"So why did you move to Roseboro?" Lela asks my parents over dinner.

My mom and dad went all out. It's our first night in the house with company, and it's clear my parents want to do it right; they've even set up the table in the dining room so we aren't eating in the kitchen like we have been. There's homemade soup and fresh salad and roast chicken with spiced potatoes and carrots. And my dad made his special chocolate chip cookies for dessert—we can smell them baking as we eat, and it's making it hard to focus on the pile of carrots that just don't seem to disappear from my plate.

My parents share a look and grin.

"Well," Mom says, "Arthur and I both grew up in the country, and we thought it was a good place to be kids. We wanted Tamal to have a similar upbringing. Get some dirt under his nails, you know?"

"Plus the cost of living is much better," Dad says. He's an accountant. He says stuff like that a lot.

"I'm sure Lela doesn't care about cost of living," Mom says with a grin. She tosses a crouton at him. He tries to catch it in his mouth and fails.

Max gives me a look that clearly asks, *Are they always like this?* and I just shrug. Because, yup, they've always been like this.

"Well, then," Dad replies, "I bet I have a topic they're *dying* to talk about." He folds his hands and rests his chin in them, looking at my new friends with a devilish glint in his bespectacled eyes. "Tell me all about this town's ghost stories."

"Arthur," Mom says, but it's clear from the sudden shifty expressions on Max's and Lela's faces that he's hit a very good subject. The other kids at my school must not be the only ones who think this place is filled with ghosts.

Chills race down my spine.

Immediately, I remember the girl I thought I saw in the hallway.

Immediately, it feels like she's watching me again.

I force down the impulse to look around and instead try to look like my heart isn't racing.

"Come on, Nadiya," Dad continues. "A small town like this has to be *brimming* with ghost stories. I mean, have you seen the abandoned mill by the river? If that isn't a hot spot of paranormal activity, I don't know what is."

Okay, so my dad's job is as an accountant. But he's also a huge supernatural buff. Like, he watches those silly ghost shows every night before bed, the ones where groups of teens go into supposedly haunted buildings with flashlights and beeping equipment they bought online and try to contact the dead. Mostly they just run around jumping at perfectly explainable noises, talking about *cold spots* and *presences* as if they aren't in a basement in Minnesota in January.

I think my dad likes them because at the end of the show, everything is inconclusive, meaning they didn't find proof of ghosts, but they still keep trying. There's always another mystery hanging in the air. There's always the chance that next time, they'll find something.

Then they'll have a real reason to be scared at what goes bump in the dark.

I watch them with him every night.

And every night, I have to force myself to pretend that walking to my bedroom alone afterward doesn't feel like the scariest thing on earth. Which is silly, because in New York, that was a very short walk.

"Well," Lela says, "there is *one* story."

"Lela, don't—" Max interjects.

"What? He asked."

My dad actually claps. My mom just rolls her eyes and leans back in her chair.

"This sounds like a good story," Dad says. "If you're not supposed to tell it."

"I guess so," Lela says. Her eyes drop to the table.

"But it's not really a story," Max says. "I mean, it *is* a story. But it's true."

"Even better," Dad says. "Where does it take place? The mill?"

Lela hesitates.

"No," she finally says. She takes a deep breath and looks straight at me. My blood runs cold—I know what she's going to say before she even speaks. "It took place here."

4

"About a hundred years ago, a real rich family moved to town," Lela says. Max angrily picks at his food, glaring at her between bites, but she ignores his silent protest.

"Up to that point, Roseboro had mostly been a farming town. But this family, the Robertsons, had big ideas. They came here to build the mill and put Roseboro on the map. I guess they thought the locals would want that, but the locals were suspicious of newcomers—especially rich newcomers—and the Robertsons weren't welcome. They weren't even allowed to build their house in the middle of town like they wanted. They were forced to build out here. Back then, this was the very outskirts, nothing but woods and fields. And the graveyard."

"Graveyard?" Dad asks. Lela's got him totally hooked.

Lela nods.

"Graveyard. Hundreds of Roseboro residents were buried here. Some people say it was just the Robertsons being spiteful, but they built their house right on top of the graveyard even though the town tried to put up a fight. They couldn't fight, really— didn't have the money. So up went the house, and then the mill. The Robertsons couldn't get anyone to work there, though. I guess they didn't expect the locals to hold a grudge so bad, or thought that they'd eventually realize that jobs were better than history. But the mill went under, and a year later so, too, did the house."

Lela goes quiet.

Dad shakes his head. "Anyone who knows anything knows not to build on a graveyard. That's rule number one."

"The real estate agent didn't happen to mention that, did she?" Mom asks, suddenly interested.

Dad shakes his head. "Not to my knowledge. Which is good, because if she had, I would have offered double!"

"*Arthur,*" Mom groans. She tosses another crouton at him. He doesn't even bother to try and catch it or swat it away. It bounces off his head and onto the floor.

"What? Just being honest. I wonder where I left all my equipment . . ."

Because yes, my dad also has ghost-hunting equipment. Most of it hasn't left the box it arrived in, but I know that he's eager to try it out. Maybe that's part of the reason he chose a mansion like this—even before knowing the story, it doesn't take a genius to imagine this place is haunted.

"Anyway," Dad continues, shaking himself of his thoughts, "I don't think this young woman was telling a *real estate* story. Where are the ghosts?"

"Besides here, you mean?" Max mutters.

Lela glares at him, then turns on the charm and smiles at my dad.

"Well," she says, "I started with the *history* of the house. But the story gets a lot darker . . ."

Dad gestures for her to continue.

I want to tell her that this is enough, that we don't need to hear any more. This isn't like watching a TV show, where we can laugh at the strangers who've willingly ventured into spooky places in search of scares. This isn't a ghost story that's happening to someone else.

She's talking about here.

The house I live in.

The house I'm stuck in.

And I don't want to know the truth.

But I can't stop her without looking like a total scaredy-cat. And that's not how I want my new friends or my dad to see me.

So I stay quiet, and Lela keeps talking, and suddenly I want nothing more than to be back in New York.

Which just shows how scared I'm getting, since no part of me has wanted to return there since we left.

"Well, this place was cursed from the very beginning," Lela says. "I mean, like you said, everyone knows not to build on a graveyard. There were issues during construction—strange noises coming from the build site, weird apparitions. I heard one of the builders was even killed. But when the family did move in, it got . . . worse."

I look down at the floor. I start to imagine the skeletons buried underneath. All the tombstones cleared away so this house could be built. In my mind's eye, the skeletons scrabble through the soil, slowly scratching their way to the surface, while the wind in the trees echoes with the howls of ghosts.

Suddenly, I'm grateful I already ate my dinner— my stomach feels like a block of ice.

Lela continues. "The owners had four kids, you see. Three boys and a girl. And the first night in the house, one of them got very sick—the youngest son. He died a few days later. The family was heartbroken and tried to do everything they could to protect the rest of their kids, but the mother got sick and died. Then, one by one, the rest of the kids followed. First the daughter, who was about our age when she passed. Then the two eldest sons. The dad eventually left town and was never seen again. But they say you can still hear someone crying out at night."

She goes silent and picks up a forkful of cold mashed potatoes.

"Oooh," Dad says. "Very creepy indeed—I can see why our realtor didn't say anything about that. We'll have to keep our ears open for crying kids. And we're just going to have to make sure Tamal takes his vitamin C every day."

He smiles at me.

But I can't smile back. I have too many questions.

What did they die of?

Could it have been stopped? I think of the girl I saw in the hall, and the worst question of all rings in my mind:

Are they still here?

Upstairs, a box crashes with a deafening thud.

We all jump, even Dad, who immediately starts laughing.

"Sounds like one of our box piles toppled," Dad says. Then he makes his voice all spooky. "Or mayyybe it was a ghoooost."

Mom snorts.

"I think it's time for dessert," she says, pushing

herself to standing. I get to my feet and help her clear the dishes while Dad prods Lela for more details.

"I don't know what gets into him sometimes," Mom says when we're in the kitchen.

I place the dishes in the sink and start rinsing them off.

"He just likes being scared," I say, not looking up from my work.

"Is it scaring you?" she asks.

I shake my head. The truth is, yes, it's creeping me out. But I don't want to tell her that. She's always been the one I went to when I was scared, always comforting me when I woke up with nightmares. I don't want her worrying about me now. She already has more than enough to deal with.

"Good." She comes over and ruffles my hair. "Come on, leave those for later. Let's eat these cookies while they're warm."

She shuffles off into the dining room, carrying the cookies with her. I hear Dad and my friends exclaim happily when she enters.

I turn off the water.

Look up into the reflection in the window above the sink.

A girl stands far behind me, on the distant side of the dining room. The girl with the teddy bear.

I jerk around.

Save for my family and friends, there's no one there.

5

Lela goes home shortly after dinner. Max and I wave to her from the front step as her parents drive her off.

My new house is up on a hill, overlooking the rest of the town, which glitters in the early evening light below. Woods stretch up and around us on all sides, making the house feel like it's completely isolated, like we're a castle in the clouds.

Except I have an eerie suspicion that my new castle is haunted, and that Max is hiding more than he's letting on. He didn't say anything about the ghost story after dinner, even when we were all playing board games together as we waited for Lela's parents to show. To be fair, Lela didn't say anything else either. But Max seemed to be desperately trying to pretend we'd never even brought the subject up.

We stand there, neither of us wanting to go inside even though it's chilly, waiting for his parents to come get him. Owls hoot far away in the woods behind us, and the lights cast from my house's windows scatter across the massive front lawn, dancing like phantoms on the grass. It's easy to imagine this place as a graveyard.

It's easy to wonder what they did with all the graves.

I focus instead on the lights down there, on all the houses filled with people. People who most definitely aren't worried about haunted houses or mysterious floating girls.

"Is that yours?" I ask, pointing the smear of flickering lights.

Max chuckles. "No," he says. "Mine's that one. Over there. By the other blinking light."

"Ooooh, right," I say. "That's what I thought." I pause. "How long have you lived here?"

"My whole life," he says. "My entire family grew up here. Same with Lela's."

It makes me think of the way everyone at school looked at me—the suspicion, and maybe even the fear. "I take it there aren't many newcomers."

He looks over to me. "Honestly, I think you guys are the first family to move here since I was born."

"Wow," I say. No wonder they knew who I was immediately.

A new question wiggles its way to my mind, even though I don't want to ask it. For some reason, I ask it anyway.

"Is that why she wanted to be friends with me? Because I live in a haunted house."

Max doesn't answer right away.

"Maybe, at first," he says slowly. He looks at me, then away. "But that was before she knew you. When we found out that someone was moving into the house on the hill, it was all anyone could talk about. Naturally she wanted to know who you were. But that's not why we're friends." He reaches over and pats my shoulder. "You're cool. We like hanging out with you. That's why we're here. Not because Lela seems to think this place is haunted."

I turn to Max.

"Do you?"

"No."

Maybe it's my imagination, but I think he's lying.

"Are you scared of this place?" I ask.

He doesn't answer at first.

"No," he finally says. "It's a scary story, but I don't think it's real. Just something some bored kids thought up to try and make this place interesting."

This time it's most definitely *not* my imagination. Max is lying. But whether he's lying about not being scared or not thinking it's real, I can't tell.

"Cool," I say. "Do you, um. Do you want to stay over tomorrow?"

Tomorrow's Saturday, and save for homework and unpacking, I'm not going to be doing anything else. It's our second weekend in the house, and I really don't want to be spending it on my own. I tell myself it's because if he's here, I won't have to keep unpacking. The truth is, I don't want to be alone.

"I don't know," he says. "I have to ask my mom."

"Right."

Silence presses down upon us, broken only by the hooting owls and the wind rustling the trees.

"You've lived here your whole life," I point out. "Does that mean . . . has anyone else ever lived here? Since the original family?"

The house didn't seem completely run-down when we moved in, though it was definitely a fixer-upper. A lot of walls had cracks and needed to be plastered and repainted. There were a few chunks missing in the upstairs ceilings. Vines clambered all over the exterior. But it's not as if we moved in to broken windows and rat nests.

Again, he hesitates.

"A few," he finally says. "No one . . ." He swallows. "No one stays here very long."

"What do you mean?" I ask.

Once more, I imagine the distant ghost girl. She'd be more than enough to scare anyone off.

"I don't like talking about it." He doesn't sound defensive—he honestly sounds scared.

"I don't really want to hear about it either," I admit. "But, I mean, this is my house. I feel like I should know what's happened here."

"Well," he says, "it's just stories, you know? But apparently, it's usually big families who move here.

Usually from the city. Because there's so much space, and the place is so cheap. A few years ago, a big family moved in. They didn't last long."

"What happened to them?"

He shrugs.

"No one really knows. I was too young to remember much. But I've heard that some of the children went missing. That the parents got super suspicious and started thinking everyone in town was after them. And they left. Left all their stuff here, too. No one heard from them again."

Left all their stuff here . . . but the house was empty when we moved in. What does that mean?

Max goes on. "It doesn't end there. Because some kids from the high school, well, they turned it into a sort of game. See how much they could steal from the house without being caught. A few would return with odds and ends, but others . . . others never came back at all. When their parents went to look for them, they weren't anywhere to be seen. They were gone. Like, permanently gone. Everyone in town thinks they just ran off to the city, because they were teenagers and this town is super boring. Not even the police did much of an investigation. They just figured the thefts were a cover story."

"I'm guessing you and Lela don't think that."

"I don't know what I believe," he says. "But every couple years, some high schoolers get brave enough and tell everyone they're going to try it again. And they go missing. Or maybe they just run away. I don't know."

"Why'd you come up here, then?" I ask. A small part of me hopes no one comes up to try and steal anything. I don't need to be worrying about ghosts *and* thieves. "If the house is cursed."

"Because I want to be your friend," he says. His voice lightens. "Same as Lela. We don't want to let some ghost stories scare us off. I mean, they're just stories. It's like those ghost shows your dad was talking about—all the weird stuff is totally explainable. It's just our imaginations getting the better of us."

The crunch of gravel makes me startle. Max's family is pulling up the driveway—I was so entranced by his story, I hadn't even noticed the car coming. He waves and hurries over to the driver's window. His mom rolls it down and smiles at the both of us.

"Can I stay over tomorrow night?" Max asks with a big grin.

"Of course," she says. "If it's okay with his parents."

I nod. I haven't asked, but I have no doubt they'll be okay with it. I didn't have many friends in New York, so I'm sure they'll be more than happy to have friends over here.

"Okay, then," Max says. We walk over to the passenger side. "I'll see you tomorrow," he says, his hand on the door. "Unless . . ."

"Unless what?" I ask.

He rolls his eyes.

"Well, apparently there was one kid who came back with a load of cool things. So much that he decided to go back a second night. That was the last time anyone saw him. But before he left, he told everyone who would listen that while he was in there, he saw a ghost. And that it was following him."

My throat freezes, and my next words come out as a croak.

"What sort of ghost?"

"You know. See-through. Floating. Girl with long hair holding a teddy bear. Cliché stuff, you know?"

The lump of ice in my throat turns my whole body to stone.

He opens the passenger door and steps inside.

"So if you see her," he says, hanging out the window, "I might have to skip. Otherwise, I'll see you tomorrow!"

It feels like my feet are frozen to the ground. I can only stand there as he and his mom drive off, leaving me on the cold gravel drive. I consider running after them. I consider yelling out the truth.

I've seen her! She's following me!

But I don't, because the final truth is one I don't even want to consider:

I'm next!

When their taillights disappear down the hill, I turn and hurry back into the house.

I keep my eyes firmly on the ground in front of me.

I don't look up to the glowing windows.

I don't see the ghost girl

but that doesn't mean she isn't there.

"That was a fun night, wasn't it, champ?" Dad asks.

"I'm surprised you didn't scare them off," Mom replies.

They're both sitting on the sofa, reading books, the TV unpacked but unplugged on the floor before them. Apparently the thing they most enjoy about being out of New York is having silence, and I think they're worried that once they plug in the TV, they'll lose it again.

"Yeah," I say. What I don't say is: *I'm worried the ghosts that haunt this place will scare them off instead.*

They okayed Max staying over the moment I got back into the house. Like I said, they're just happy I have friends for once.

I should be happy, too. But instead of letting the stories be stories and life be life, I keep having to mix up the two. Because I can't help but ask my parents the one question that's burning brightest in my mind.

I try to make it sound casual when I ask, "What do you know about the people who lived here before us?"

"Your friends' stories have you asking questions now?" Dad asks with a grin.

I settle on the sofa between them.

"I'm just curious. I mean, they said the place was abandoned, right? But it's not like it was falling apart when you bought it."

"No," Mom says. "The real estate agency took control of the house a couple years ago, and they renovated it a little bit to appeal to new buyers."

"But what about the previous owners?" I swallow, and my voice goes quiet. "What about all that stuff about this being built on a graveyard?"

"That was all made up," Mom says. She reaches over and rubs my back. "This house wasn't built on a graveyard. They would have had to tell us that when we bought it. Right, Arthur?"

But Dad doesn't answer right away. In fact, he hesitates and bites his lip.

"I'm not so certain," he admits. "I mean, they should have. But now that I think about it . . . Don't you think they seemed a little eager to sell?"

"Arthur . . ."

"What? I'm just saying. They practically gave us the house when we asked to tour. I thought they were just trying to get some new blood in the town, but maybe they were hiding something and wanted to get the papers signed before we found out. It's not like we asked a lot of questions. Maybe it *was* built on a graveyard and they didn't want us to find out."

"Now you're just being ridiculous."

Dad shrugs. "All I know is, when I researched, I found out the house was built around the same time as the mill, so Lela's story lines up."

"But even if it *was* built on a graveyard—which it wasn't!—it doesn't mean the place is haunted or anything like that," Mom says. "I'm sure a lot of houses in these old New England towns are built on old grave-yards, and you don't hear about them being haunted!"

I can tell Dad is unnerved. His eyebrows are fur-rowed as he stares into space, thinking.

"Don't you? I mean, we've all seen the shows."

"Oh, *really*," Mom growls. "Are you trying to scare him?" She squeezes my shoulder. "Listen, Tamal. Those shows on TV are all made up. They're scripted. There aren't such things as haunted houses. No matter what your father says. If there were, don't you think people would make a bigger deal over it? There'd be reports all over the news, and you'd be taking classes in ghosts and hauntings. It's all. Made. Up."

Dad grunts. I can tell a part of him wants to argue—they've done it before, Mom saying that Dad has an overactive imagination, him saying she's close-minded, but the arguments have always been joking. This, though . . . this is getting to him.

It's one thing to joke and argue about other peo-ple's houses being haunted, and another to think it could be your own.

"I'm not saying the house is haunted," Dad finally

relents. "I'm just saying it's entirely possible that it was built on a graveyard and covered up."

"Well, if you're that concerned, we can ask the agent in the morning. But it doesn't matter. No matter the house's history, it's our home now, and I for one would rather focus on making it as comfortable as possible than digging up the past.

"Speaking of," she continues, "we all need to get some sleep. We've got a big day of unpacking and organizing tomorrow. Especially if you want to have a friend over tomorrow night."

I groan. Sleep is the last thing on my mind right now. I want to go online and research the history of the house—but we don't have internet yet, and my cell signal is spotty. I want to run down to the basement and dig at the dirt floor to see if there are tombstones. I want to be sure—once and for all—that this place isn't haunted. That the stories were just stories, and my family and I are all completely safe.

"You heard your mom," Dad says. "Bedtime, Bozo."

"Fiiine," I mutter. I shift from the sofa and give him a hug, then go over to Mom.

"Do you want me to come upstairs with you?" Mom whispers as she hugs me.

I bristle at the question. Partly because I'm not a little kid and I hate that she still thinks she needs to ask it. But mostly because yes, yes I do.

Mom knows I'm scared of the dark. She knows I'm scared of a lot of things, which is why I watch those silly ghost shows with Dad because hopefully they'll help desensitize me or something and I won't be scared anymore. She doesn't seem to realize, though, that this time the fear might be warranted. In fact, she seems to be trying very hard to convince us all of the opposite. I can't let myself believe it's all a story, though. I *know* what I've seen. I know that pretending it isn't real won't make it go away.

"No," I say. I try to smile and not look scared or insulted, though I feel a strange mix of both. There might have been a moment when I would have asked her to tuck me into bed. But now that she's asked, I can't let myself look like a little kid and agree. "Good night. Love you."

Mom smiles at me, and I turn and head up the stairs to my bedroom.

Thankfully, the lights are all already on, which means I don't have to admit that I'm scared by turning on the hall lights.

I'm torn between running up the steps at full speed just so I can get to the safety of my room and wanting to stall down here, where my parents are, where it's safe.

Well, safer.

Even though it's true that the house has been fixed up, it's still nowhere near perfect. The walls have been repainted white, and maybe it's the light or maybe it's another layer behind the white, but the crisp white color is already starting to yellow and chip in places. I head up the stairs, up the threadbare floral carpet that— even though we've vacuumed a dozen times—still looks a little dirty. My hand trails along the wooden banister as I stare at the spaces in the wall where nails jut out, the faint outline of picture frames embedded in the paint. Without any art, the place looks almost like a hospital . . . from a hundred years ago.

I pause when I reach the upstairs hall.

Half the bulbs along the wall are bare, and the

others are shrouded in old red lampshades. A few of them flicker, sending eerie shadows over the carpet and bare walls.

I really, truly don't want to walk down there.

But my bedroom is near the end of the hall, past multiple closed doors that look like they could slam open at any moment, revealing a horror within—the ghost girl, perhaps, or skeletons climbing out of the closets, or zombies crawling from the floorboards, or worse . . .

I take a deep breath.

"Get ahold of yourself," I tell myself. "This is just a hall. Just your house. You live here now, and there's no use being scared of what you can't change."

I walk a bit farther, and the flickering light makes me pause as something on the wall catches my eye. Curving shadows within the space where a painting once hung.

I lean in closer.

Then yelp and leap back.

HERE LIES THE BODY
OF ELIAS SMITH

The words are etched into the wall, the same font as on a tombstone.

I take another step backward. The light flickers again, and this time when I glance down the hall, all the walls are covered in tombstone inscriptions.

REST IN PEACE

                                        IN MEMORIAM

                  HERE LIES AMELIA

             WE WILL MISS YOU

                    FOREVER IN OUR HEARTS

I slap a hand to my mouth to keep myself from screaming out, because as the words come into focus, as the flickering lights get more intense, I see *movement* behind the chipped white paint.

Hands pressing against the boards.

Faces, mouths open in silent screams, stretching the old wallpaper.

I stumble backward, trip, and fall to the carpet.

When I look back, the hallway is empty, the lights steady. No sign of the tombstones. No sign of the bodies trying to get out.

It must have been my imagination.

There's no way that just happened.

Except my heart is hammering so loud in my ears I can't hear anything else. My hands shake violently as I push myself up to standing. I lean against the wall, then jerk away when I remember what was behind it only moments ago.

I take a deep breath and try to talk myself out of having a freak-out.

It's just your imagination, I say in my head. *There's no ghost. This house isn't haunted. You're not a little kid anymore, and that means you shouldn't be frightened of the dark.*

It takes all my self-control not to run to the end of the hall. Not to call out for Mom or Dad to come up here and tuck me in because I'm not brave enough to be upstairs alone in my own house after all.

Step by step, I make my way to the end of the hall. To where my room waits.

The walls don't move.

The tombstone inscriptions don't reappear.

I reach the door.

The open door. It should have been closed. I *know* it was closed.

I turn to go inside.

Before I do, I look over my shoulder. Back toward the stairs. Back toward the hall, where the zombies appeared.

It's no longer empty.

The ghost girl hovers at the far end of the hall, her toes inches from the ground.

She's about the same distance away from me that she was in the dining room.

My heart stops.

"M—" I stammer. "Mom?"

The girl doesn't move.

Just hovers there. Black hair covering her face.

Behind that veil, I know, she smiles.

I blink, and when my eyes open again, she is closer.

Just an inch.

I run into my room and slam the door shut.

I wait.

I reach out my hand and flip on the lights.
I don't move from the door.
I wait.
And wait.
And wait.

Eventually, after what feels like hours have passed, there's a knock on my door.

thud

thud

thud

I yelp and dart away, but a moment later, my mom's voice calls out, "Tamal, honey, are you still awake?"

Immediately, I leap into bed and pull up the covers.

"What?" I ask, trying to make my voice sound like I just woke up.

She opens the door and steps in.

"What are you doing with all the lights on?" she says. "It's way past your bedtime."

"I fell asleep."

"With the lights on?"

"I . . . I forgot."

She looks at me knowingly and takes a step inside.

"You *forgot*. Does that have anything to do with the stories your friends were telling tonight?"

I look away.

"No," I lie.

She comes over and sits on the side of my bed, putting a hand on my shoulder.

"Those are just stories, sweetheart," she says. "This house isn't haunted, I promise you. People just like making up ghost stories to explain things that they can't understand."

I nod. It's not the first time we've had a talk like this. It definitely won't be the last. Unless, of course, the ghost girl gets me.

I hear Mom take a deep breath.

"Besides," she says, "if there *were* ghosts in here—which there aren't!—your dad and I would scare them away. Promise."

I try to smile when I look at her. She smiles back, then kisses the top of my head. In that moment, I want nothing more than to tell her what I've seen. The ghost girl. The hallway with its tombstones. But I also know that she won't believe me. She'll think it was an overactive imagination from all the stories. She'll just tell me once more that she can keep the ghosts away.

Even though I have a deep, dark feeling that she can't.

"Get some sleep," she says. "You've got a big day tomorrow! Your first sleepover in our new house. We'll need to unpack some things to make it more comfortable for Max, and I'll need your help."

"Okay, Mom," I say.

She stands and walks to the door, flipping off the light before she leaves.

She keeps the door open.

"Mom?" I ask before she goes too far.

"Yes, sweetheart?"

"Can you shut the door?"

She smiles again.

"Of course."

She closes the door gently behind her. I hear her

walk down the hall. I don't hear her scream out in terror. If the ghost girl is waiting, my mother doesn't see her.

It doesn't make me feel much better.

Neither does the closed door.

A few weeks ago, Dad and I watched a documentary about a family that moved out of their haunted mansion because their youngest daughter said her toys were floating around and talking to her at night. They thought the house was haunted, so after consulting psychics and ghost hunters, they left.

And the ghost followed them.

And followed them.

Until they died of fright.

If there's one thing I learned, it's that nothing can stop a ghost that wants to get you.

Nothing.

9

In my dreams, she is following me.

I'm at the playground, swinging with my friends, who have no faces, and when I look over, she is there, at the edge of the playground, just beyond the swing set. Except she is closer, so much closer, and when I look to my friends and look back to her, she is only feet away. I leap from the swing set and fly through the air, and when I land, I'm on the beach, running through the sand, but every step makes me sink a little deeper, and the waves are crashing a little higher, and someone is laughing, laughing so hard and so evilly that chills race over my skin despite the burning sun. When I look over my shoulder, she is there, gaining on me, her feet brushing trails into the sand. I yell and look forward and run faster, but the moment I turn, she is in front of me, and I stumble, fall to my hands and knees in the waves. I scramble to standing and start swimming in the pool, sloshing forward toward the stairs at the far end, because the ghost is behind me, hovering above the water. I yell out to the lifeguards, but they aren't looking.

No.

They are *her*. The ghost with the long black hair, a teddy bear in her hand. Everywhere I turn, she is there, getting closer, and when I look behind me again, she floats only feet away. I tread water and feel cold hands grasp at my feet. I slosh, barely able to keep my head up, and I am sinking, sinking, and when I see her reflection in the water, it's not just a girl but an old man in coveralls, and around him are dozens of ghostly children, and he raises his hand and points at me and his eyes glow red as he mouths, *Take him!* and the kids rush me and grab my ankles and push my head down, and as the water sloshes into my lungs and I sink, I see her before me, the ghost girl with the teddy bear. Her hair billows around her underwater. I can see her face. Her sad, terrifying face.

She reaches out her hands and grabs my neck . . .

10

I wake with my heart racing, fully expecting to see the ghost girl in front of me.

But my room is free of apparitions, and after a few minutes of slow breathing, my dream fades, and so, too, does the panic. The longer I sit there, the harder it is to imagine being scared.

After all, the sun is out and birds are chirping and from downstairs I can faintly hear my parents listening to their favorite podcast. The light streaming in makes my huge room look serene—the wood floors, the piles of boxes, the stacks of books in corners, the light dancing off dust motes in the air. Everything is crisp and open—a fresh start. A new beginning. And tonight, I'm going to have Max over for a sleepover, and there won't be any scary stories or bad dreams, just games and fun. I settle back on my bed and just sit there for a moment, letting my dream fade to nothing. As it does, I start to feel silly, especially in the light of day.

I shouldn't have let my imagination take over again. Or let Lela's story take root in my brain.

There was no ghost in the house, just like Mom said. We weren't built on a graveyard—surely, someone would have told us that before we bought the place.

We're safe.

I'm safe.

Slightly emboldened, I roll out of bed and put on my brand-new slippers. With every second, my heart gets a little lighter. Maybe it's from the sunlight, or maybe it's just my newfound belief that all the fears from last night were unfounded.

I wander down the hall, humming to the music.

When I reach the top of the stairs, I stop.

The hairs on the back of my neck stand on end.

I turn.

And there, floating in front of my room in a shaft of sunlight, glimmering just like the dust motes and just as insubstantial and ever present, is the ghost girl.

She's closer than ever before.

All happiness, all assurance that everything is okay, vanishes like a popped balloon.

"Who . . . who are you?" I ask. The words tremble in my throat.

The girl doesn't answer. Her head tilts to the side.

I blink and step back, and she is a foot closer.

I don't wait around. I turn and run.

II

A part of me wants to tell my parents what I've seen.

But when I get down to the first floor, panting from running all the way there, and see them laughing and unpacking in the kitchen, I realize I can't. Not just because I feel silly. Not just because I'm not entirely certain the ghost isn't just in my imagination. But because they actually look happy. I mean, they were always happy together, but they were stressed out, too. They've seemed relaxed since we moved here, and I don't want to be the reason we have to leave here and go back to the city.

So I don't tell them anything. It feels like lying. It feels *dangerous*.

We have breakfast, and they unpack a bit more as I eat my cereal. I have a few hours before Max is going to show up, and it's too early to want to do homework. I could hook up the TV, but I don't want to stay inside and I *definitely* don't want to go up to my room to unpack on my own. Even though I don't see the ghost all through breakfast, I can't let myself believe that she isn't there. That feels more dangerous than anything else.

When I'm done eating, I stand and somewhat help them unpack. I hand dishes to Mom half-heartedly, while Dad goes into the living room to start shifting around the furniture.

"Are you feeling okay?" Mom asks.

I shrug and hand her a stack of small plates.

She takes the plates and sets them on the counter, then gently takes my chin in her hand and raises my face to look at her. She clucks her tongue in a worried sort of way.

"You look exhausted. Are you having trouble sleeping again?"

There's no use pretending. Besides, it's better that she thinks I'm out of it because of nightmares and not because I'm worried there's a ghost in the house.

"Bad dreams," I admit.

"I'm going to have to have a talk with your father," she mutters. "No more scary movies for a while. Or stories. I have a feeling he's going to try to get your friend to tell us more about the history of this place."

"It's okay, really."

"It's not, honey," she says. "This is our home now. It's a big change even without worrying about ghosts or whatever nonsense the locals made up. I don't want you worrying yourself sick."

She sounds so concerned, a part of me wants to admit everything—I've been seeing a ghost, I'm worried the stories are true—while the other part is almost offended. She's talking to me like I'm a little kid.

And yes, maybe I'm still scared of the dark, and maybe I am worried about a ghost in this house, but I can still take care of myself.

She must notice all the conflicting thoughts in my head, because she leans in to hug me before standing.

"Why don't you go play outside?" Mom suggests. "Some fresh air will be good for you, and I'll have a word with your father."

I nod and head out to the front yard. As the door closes behind me, I distinctly hear her call out, *"Arthur!"*

The remaining leaves on the trees surrounding us are orange and red, and there's a crisp scent in the air that's unlike anything I ever smelled in New York. It smells like fresh dirt and leaves—completely different from the usual exhaust and trash of the city.

In that moment, it's once more hard to believe that this place is haunted.

Our house stretches up behind me, all white walls and big glittering windows. The ivy engulfing the walls is as green as the pine trees that encircle us; the vines lend a sort of mystery to the house, as if the earth itself is trying to shroud it in secret. From afar, the house looks grand and imposing, but this close, it's easy to see that it isn't as magical as it once was. There are tiles missing from the roof, and spider-webs in the corners of the windows, and the white siding is peeled or flaking off in places. Not for the first time, I wonder why the original family built something so large. How could one family need so much space? And, for that matter, why did we? Dad said we got the place because it was so cheap, but I don't think we need this much house. Surely there were places in Roseboro itself that were smaller and cheaper.

It makes me wonder if he had an inkling that this place might be haunted. I mean, it fit the bill perfectly: monstrously large, abandoned for years, and isolated on a hillside away from the town. Even if he didn't know about the graveyard, I wonder if he had hoped this place might hold some secrets.

I wonder if he knows just how right he was.

Something flickers in a top window. My heart leaps to my throat, but before I can freak out, I realize that it's clouds reflecting off the glass. I take a deep breath and try to steady my nerves.

Whatever reason we're here, it's clear that I need to find the truth.

I need to find out for myself if the story that Lela told was true.

I think I know just how to do it.

12

Even though the house and front yard are huge, the backyard is kind of small. There's a tiny back patio and maybe five feet of grassy lawn that stretches around the house, but beyond that is a tall, gnarled hedge and the sprawl of thick forest right behind. It's almost like the builders couldn't be bothered to clear away the forest that encroaches on all sides.

Either that, or they were scared by it.

I poke around the backyard. Lela had said this place was built on a graveyard, and that's what I'm hoping to find. If there aren't any graves, then maybe I can convince myself that the rest of the story was made up as well. No graveyard, no curse, no ghosts. Right? Just a big old house on a hill, and a bunch of stories that have made me believe in impossible things.

At first, I don't find anything unusual. The back-yard hasn't been mowed for a while, and the tall grass reaches up to my knees. Rocks litter the yard as well, and it takes a lot of concentration not to stumble over them as I walk. But I bend over and pick up a few, just to make sure, and see that they are indeed just normal rocks. Not crumbled graves or anything remotely scary.

I even look under the patio, though I don't see anything in the tiny crawl space beyond shadows and spiderwebs and what looks like a very old-fashioned lawn mower. I don't peer under there long. Who knows what wild animals are living under there.

After twenty minutes, I've surveyed the entire yard, front and back. I sit on the edge of the patio, looking up at the hedge and the trees beyond. Birds sing in the forest, and squirrels scamper from branch to branch.

Perfectly peaceful.

"Nothing there," I say to myself. No graves. No clues. No curses. My heart lifts just a little bit.

It was just a story, after all.

Just as I push myself to standing, though, I see it.

A break in the hedge.

The shadow of a path.

Easy to miss if you aren't looking at it straight on.

I don't know why, but it feels like a hook latches on just behind my rib cage, cold and powerful. I can't shake it, nor can I shake the chills that race over me despite the warm daylight.

The hook tugs me forward. Toward the trail.

Without even a backward glance to see if my parents are watching from the kitchen window, I follow.

13

I expect the path to be tangled and overgrown, but gravel crunches underfoot as I pass through the narrow space in the hedge. The path meanders through the woods, twining between trees with thick trunks, so after a few steps—when I look over my shoulder—I can't even see my own house anymore.

Suddenly, I realize that the whole forest has gone quiet, like it's holding its breath.

Maybe I should turn around, I think.

But then, as if my thinking brought it about, I step around a tree and see a tiny, abandoned area full of tombstones.

It's maybe only the size of my room, if not smaller, with a sad, rusted wire fence encircling it. I pause. All the tombstones are so old and weathered that I can't make out anything on the faces, and they're piled on top of each other, so they can't possibly be matched with graves anymore. It's almost like they were tossed here, some upright and others just in mounds. This clearly isn't an original graveyard. This feels like an afterthought.

A dumping ground.

As if . . . as if these tombstones were all relocated out here, in the middle of the woods, far away from their original resting places.

In the center is a monument. One that makes my heart stop beating.

It's a tiny mausoleum, a stone shed the size of a doghouse. Just large enough to hold a child-sized coffin within. The door on the front is dead-bolted shut. But on top, towering high above me, is a statue.

A statue of a girl.

A girl with long hair falling past her shoulders, and a teddy bear held between her hands.

The statue's face is tilted back, a smile on her

smooth stone lips, as if she's basking in the ray of sunlight that streaks down through the trees, alighting on her face.

Even though the statue is serene, it fills me with dread.

I know in my heart that it is the same girl I've seen in the hallways.

The same ghost that is slowly stalking me.

My friends had been telling the truth—there *was* a graveyard on our property. I don't understand who moved the markers all the way out here or why all the tombstones look broken, save for the one of the little girl.

There's no way I could have made up a ghost that looked exactly like this girl.

The ghost is real.

The ghost is real, and until I find out what she wants, I know without doubt she won't rest until I join her in the grave.

14

"Tell me more about the family who had this house built," I ask Max. "The original owners."

We're sitting up in my room, a TV and game system set up before us, and we haven't really spoken much since Max got here an hour ago. Not that we're ignoring each other, but it's hard to talk when trying to not lose the game. Max keeps losing, but not because he's a bad player—he was the one who recommended we play this fighting game, and said he was really good at it. I believe him. But I also can tell he's distracted.

I know he's trying to hide it from me, but I keep seeing him glance behind us nervously when he thinks I'm not looking.

As if he's watching for a ghost.

He startles when I ask him. On-screen, his character falls off a ledge. GAME OVER.

"What do you want to know?" he asks me while making it clear he'd rather be talking about something else.

"Lela said that their kids had died, including the daughter. Do you . . . do you know what she looks like?"

Max swallows.

"Why would I know that?" he asks. He tries to say it nonchalantly, but I catch the note of fear in his voice. "It was a long time ago."

"Because . . . because she's the one that's haunting this place, isn't she? She's the one the kids who raided this place saw before they went missing."

Max freezes.

"How did—?"

"I've seen her," I admit.

He drops the controller and doesn't pick it up.

Instead, he stares at me with wide, fear-filled eyes.

"You what?"

"At least, I think I've seen her," I say. My voice picks up speed, like a dam bursting over its banks—I don't want him to stop me, or to give him the chance to think I'm losing it. "The last couple nights. And just this morning I went out into the woods behind the house and found a bunch of tombstones and a statue that looked just like her. She had long black hair and floated a few inches off the ground—"

"And carried a teddy bear in her hand," Max finishes.

The breath catches in my throat.

"Yeah," I reply. "How did you know?"

"Because that's how all the stories go. Have you . . . have you seen her face?"

I shake my head. My palms instantly go clammy as he confirms all my worst fears. She's real. Other people have seen her, which means she's real.

And after they saw her, they disappeared.

"No," I finally manage to say. "Her face is always hidden by her hair. And she's always like twenty feet away from me."

I don't tell him that I've noticed she's getting slowly, steadily closer.

"Good," he says firmly. "You need to keep it that way."

"What do you mean?"

"I mean . . ." He takes a deep breath. When he looks away, I think maybe I've lost him, that he'll refuse to tell the rest of the tale. "The kids that came back said that she stalks her victims. For days or weeks. And when she finally decides to take you, she shows you her face. And then . . . then you disappear."

"Disappear?"

He nods gravely.

"The town tries to keep it hushed up. But we've heard the rumors. It wasn't just the kids who came to steal from this place. Apparently . . . apparently she appeared to the kids who moved here. And then, after a while, they would vanish as well. It's why the place has been empty so long. No one stays here. No one wants to move back. It's too risky."

He looks at me, and the unspoken truth falls heavy between us:

She's appeared to me. Just as she appeared to the kids who moved here or stole from here.

And that means I don't have much time.

Soon, she'll show me her face.

And I will never be seen again.

15

"Show me," Lela says.

Max called her right away, and she biked all the way up from town to get here. There's a light sheen of sweat on her forehead, but even though she just arrived, it's clear she's ready for action. She can't spend the night, but so long as she's home by dinner, we can explore my creepy home together.

And honestly, she seems like the only one brave enough to do any actual exploring—Max and I have stayed safely outside the house since he told me the truth about the ghost. Even though she had gotten here as soon as she could, it still felt like it had taken forever.

I still spent the entire time waiting for the ghost to appear in the windows, her eyes wide and mouth open in a silent scream right before she grabbed me.

I poke along the back hedge with a stick, trying to find the opening and gravel trail I'd seen before, while Max and Lela trade stories behind me. I try not to listen in, but it's impossible not to hear. Especially because Lela doesn't seem nearly as hesitant to talk about the haunting of my house—or my potential impending doom—as Max.

"Well, *I* heard her face was a skull," she says, "and that kids didn't go missing—they were so scared when they saw her, they *died*."

I feel both of them pause and stare at me when she says it. I don't turn around.

"I never heard that," Max says quietly. I can tell he's no longer sure what he believes.

All I know is that I need to get to the bottom of this. I need to learn as much about who lived in this house as I can. Worst-case scenario—the house is haunted, and I need to find a way to get rid of the ghost. Best-case scenario—the house *isn't* haunted, and in learning the true history, I can put all these ghost stories to rest.

The first step is exploring the gravestones and learning *who* exactly was buried there, and why they were dumped in the middle of the woods.

Then I can also find out who lived and died here once the house was built.

Maybe if I can learn the girl's name, I can figure out why she's haunting my halls.

After a few more minutes of walking back and forth along the hedges, though, I can't find the path.

"I'm sure it was here!" I say, tossing my stick down in frustration.

"Maybe it's overgrown," Max says. Right—like somehow the hedges just magically grew to cover the space in a matter of hours.

"Or maybe *she* doesn't want you to find it," Lela says. She pauses and considers. "Or maybe she doesn't want *us* to find it."

I swallow.

"So you believe it was here?" I ask. "You don't think I was just making it up?"

"There are easier ways to get attention," Lela says. "Unless you're hinting that we shouldn't trust you?"

I shake my head. "No, no. It was here. I'm just . . . I'm surprised you believe me."

"Of course we believe you," Max says. "You live in a haunted house."

He says it so matter-of-factly, a part of me wishes he'd be doubtful. The fact that they both believe me so easily hammers in a reality I never thought I'd have to face—the house is haunted. For real. And that means I'm in danger. For real.

I look between the two of them.

"If we can't find the gravestones," I say, "we need to go someplace that might have information on this house."

"The internet?" Max asks.

"I've already tried," I admit. "I checked on my phone; there's nothing."

I hadn't spent the time between finding the gravestones and Max's arrival just sitting around. I'd searched for everything I could on this house, but there was nothing online. It made me a little less frustrated with Dad—if *I* couldn't find anything about this dark place's history while explicitly searching for it, how would he have found it when just looking up real estate stats?

"The library, then?" Max suggests.

I nod.

"Ugh, fine," Lela says. "But I'm not biking all the way back down there again. I just caught my breath!"

16

If my parents are confused by the fact that we ask to go into town less than thirty minutes after Lela's arrived, they don't show it. Probably because I'm quick to point out that we want to go to the library. On a Saturday. I tell them it's so we can do some homework, but I can tell there's no point trying to explain—Dad's halfway to the car before I even finish my request.

Like I said, they're really, really happy I have friends. Their enthusiasm is almost kind of depressing.

"So," Dad says as we make our way down the drive. He looks over to Lela, who I let take the front seat, while Max and I sit in the back. Her bike is stashed safely on the rack. "Will you be researching any new scary stories at the library?"

I tense up and dart a glance at Max, who looks just as shocked as me—did Dad overhear us talking in the yard?

Lela just laughs it off.

She tells my dad, "Only if you think our teacher is a zombie. Which he might be. Mr. Barnes is *really* old."

Dad chuckles and makes small talk, asking her about her favorite subjects and what sports she plays. I mostly zone out, keeping my ears perked for mention of ghosts or graveyards. Nothing. Until . . .

"You remember the story I told you last night, right?" Lela asks.

"Of course," Dad replies. "Hard to forget."

"Well . . . are you mad that the people who sold you the house didn't tell you about any of that?"

"Nope. Although I think if they did I might have offered even more than what they were asking! I mean, the chance to live in a real haunted house? How cool is that?"

"Very cool," she replies. She glances at me in the rearview. I try to psychically ask her not to say anything else, but of course she doesn't hear me. "So, um, have you seen anything?"

My dad just smiles.

"Nope. No luck just yet. I hope so, though. I'm still trying to find all my ghost-hunting equipment. Once I do, you kids are going to have to come over for another sleepover, and we can test it all out. Who knows, maybe we'll be the next viral sensation!" He chuckles to himself, as though this is all just a game and not a matter of life and death.

Which, I suppose, it is to him. He hasn't seen the ghost. He isn't in danger.

"What about you, Tamal?" he continues. "Seen any ghosts wandering our hallways?"

It's like ice gets lodged in my throat. I can't talk. I can't believe he asked me that.

I want to say yes, yes I have. I want him to believe me, to know that I'm not just scared—I'm in danger—and then he'll sell the house and we can move back somewhere safer.

But I don't. Because he would think I was just making it up, or that my imagination was getting the better of me. Or, worse—and even more likely—he'd get excited that I'd seen a ghost. He'd want to hunt it. Even though I was in danger. He'd say it was all okay, no one *really* went missing, a ghost couldn't *really* hurt me. He'd see it as his chance to prove that ghosts were real. Even though, for me, this ghost is a real threat.

I don't say anything. I don't know what's worse—Dad believing me and trying to get involved, or him not believing me and thinking I'm overreacting to a new house. I decide that the best thing I can do is just try to solve this on my own. That way, he never has to worry about the danger.

That way, he can continue to view ghosts as silly entertainment.

"No," I finally croak. "No ghosts here."

I stare out the window and try to force down my dread. Even my friends see this as a game. They don't feel hunted like I do.

What I see outside the window makes my heart stop dead.

The ghost girl.

At the far end of the lane.

Translucent but visible, even in the bright light of day.

The ghost girl is following me.

Even outside my home.

And she is getting closer.

17

"I saw her," I say the moment Dad drives off. We stand just outside the library—a small brick building in the heart of the tiny downtown. There are only a few people wandering about. I don't think I've ever been somewhere so quiet.

"Where?" Lela asks.

"A few blocks from here. I looked out the window and saw her down the road."

"Are you *sure* it was her?" Max asks.

"Of course."

"Maybe it was your reflection?" he presses, though

it's clear he knows it's not the case. "With, like, hair in your face."

I shake my head. "And me carrying a teddy bear I didn't notice was in my hand?"

Max swallows and looks around, as if expecting to see the ghost himself. But she isn't anywhere to be seen. I almost want the ghost to show up. I almost want to see if she appears to them, too. At least then I won't feel so strangely alone. Even though my friends say they believe me, I know they won't fully until they see her themselves.

"What did she look like?" Lela asks matter-of-factly. She stands from locking up her bike.

I tell her, and she nods as I talk, as though I'm describing an interesting bird or cloud.

"That sounds like the ghost, all right," Lela confirms. It doesn't make me feel any better. "But I didn't realize she could leave the house." She looks to Max. "All the stories I've heard say she was confined to the hallways."

"Apparently the stories weren't entirely true," I respond. "Because she's out here. She could be anywhere."

"Do you see her now?" Max asks timidly.

I shake my head before I even look around to confirm—I'd rather pretend she's not here than discover she is.

"I wonder if she'll show up again," Lela ponders. "Do you think you could call her?"

"What?" I ask incredulously. "You want me to *try* and get the ghost to appear?"

She shrugs. I can't help but think that she seems excited about all of this. Doesn't she understand the danger I'm in?

"It's just a thought," she says. "Maybe we could communicate. Figure out what she wants."

"I tried that already," I reply. "It didn't work. If anything, I think it made her mad."

"If only we knew her name . . ." Lela mutters. I don't want to know why she wants to know the ghost's name. I don't want to get on a first-name basis with the spirit hunting me.

"We should get inside," Max says. He looks around. Even though it's fairly warm out, his arms are wrapped around himself tightly. At least I don't have to worry about *him* trying to make friends with the ghost. "We have to stop you from being next."

"Yeah," Lela says. "Let's see what we can find out."

We head into the library, and as we go, I realize two things.

One, Lela is *way* too excited about seeing this ghost for herself.

And two, if we don't discover the truth quickly, the ghost following me won't be the only one haunting this town.

18

The library is two floors of sprawling bookshelves, and computers that look older than I am. After asking the helpful librarian, we find ourselves up in the back shelves, in a section of local history that is filled with dust-covered books that I'm pretty certain no one but the author ever actually read. The three of us sit there, books spread out on the floor, poring through indexes and skimming chapter headlines for any reference to my new house and the family who built it.

"I'm going to go check the computers," Lela says after setting aside yet another dusty tome. "I think they have all the old papers saved somewhere. I bet I can find something there."

We nod, though I barely look up from the book I'm reading to watch her go. A few more minutes pass. Every second that goes by without finding something feels like another failure, another step closer to my eventual disappearance. For as big of a house as it is, and with all the local lore, there is *nothing* about the original owners anywhere. Not even records of a graveyard on the hill. It's like all record of what happened up there vanished.

Just like I'm about to.

Max slams his book shut, making me jolt. The dust cloud causes him to start sneezing. He sneezes so loudly and so many times that I'm worried he's going to pass out.

"Sorry," he says between sneezes. "I'll be right back." And he jumps up, covering his nose with his elbow and sneezing the whole way down the hall.

I chuckle and watch him run off to the bathroom, but the humor fades quickly. We've been here for what feels like ages, and we're no closer to finding the truth. A part of me wants to yell and throw books, and another wants to break down crying, and another just wants to run away.

Even though I know deep down that running away won't help.

The ghost can follow me anywhere.

I flip through the chapter headings without even really seeing them, when movement from the corner of my eye catches my attention. It must just be Lela or Max coming back, because no one else would wander into this part of the library.

Except a few seconds pass, and the figure hasn't come any closer.

I freeze.

And slowly

look

over

to see the ghost girl hovering at the end of the aisle.

She is closer now. Maybe only fifteen feet away. I can see the individual tufts of fur on her teddy bear, the frayed hem of her dress.

"What . . . what do you want from me?" I stammer. "Why are you following me?"

She doesn't answer. She doesn't move. She just hovers there, light streaming through her transparent body, her bear held loosely in one hand. Maybe Lela is right—maybe there's a way to communicate. Maybe I can convince her that I'm not trying to, I don't know, take over her house or whatever. Maybe then she'll leave me alone.

"I saw your grave," I continue. "We're trying to find out what happened to you. My friends and me. We want to help. Max and Lela and me. We're all here to help you."

And maybe it's my imagination, but I swear her head tilts to the side a fraction of an inch. Like she hears me. Like it's registering.

"No one can help me," a voice whispers in my mind, so faint I think it's my imagination. A young girl's voice, lost and sad. Then the voice hardens, grows louder. *"And no one can help you!"*

I blink.

And she is inches closer.

Her free hand is out, fingers clawed, grasping toward my face.

I yelp, push myself backward, tumbling over the books, unable to take my eyes off her.

Unable to blink, for fear she'll move closer. Can she only move when I'm not looking? Is this some terrible game of cat and mouse?

"No!" I yelp. "Stay away!"

Then Max steps around the corner, through her body, and she dissolves like mist in the sunlight.

19

"She's here?" yelps Max after seeing my face.

"Shh!" Lela hisses, coming over quickly. She glances around, but we're secluded enough that no one is listening in, or upset that Max is being too loud.

"Yeah," I say. I point to the end of the aisle. "She was right over there." I look at Max. "And then you walked through her."

Max shivers, even though there's no ghost and no breeze.

"I didn't even see her," he says, his voice timid.

"That's because she's not after you," Lela says

matter-of-factly. She strides over and hands me a printout. "Here. I found this in the collection. There wasn't much, but it's something."

Max crowds near as we all look down at the printout, which is a copy of an old newspaper clipping. In a blurry font, it reads

MISERY AT THE MILL

Only three days after its opening, rumors abound that the Robertson Family Mill will be closing its doors in the coming week. After repeated family tragedies—which included the death of Herbert Robertson's wife and his two youngest children—those closest to Mr. Robertson say his grief prevents him from working. His two eldest boys have not been seen since their mother's death, and it is feared that they, too, are ill.

"Serves them right," says one local. "They never should have built here. We don't want people like them in town, or their business. No respect for history."

Whether or not the mill will close is yet to be seen. It currently employs only five workers, none of whom were available for comment.

I read the article a few more times. Lela is right—there isn't much there. But it confirms that the history surrounding the ghost stories was true.

"So there *was* a family that lost their children, including their daughter," I whisper. I look up at them. This makes it even more real.

But the part that sticks with me is the quoted local. *Serves them right.* What family deserves such tragedy? Lela's story made it sound like the Robertsons were the bad guys for building on the graveyard and meddling with the town, but the article's tone is almost making me think they might have also been victims.

"Is there anything at all about the land it was on?" I ask. "Anything about the graveyard being torn down, or the workers dying?"

Lela shakes her head. "Nothing. I would have thought there would have been an uproar about it in the paper, but if there was, I couldn't find it."

"So all we know is that the Robertsons were real, and that they had the mill, and they lived in the house. And that three of them died there."

They both nod.

"And nothing about the other kids that went missing later on?"

"Just local legend," Lela says. "If there are any records of what happened, it looks like they're gone."

"Or destroyed," Max chimes in. "Someone doesn't want us to know what's happening."

"Or some*thing*," Lela adds.

I sigh.

It feels like hitting a dead end.

With the ghost getting closer, that's not the only end I know I'm reaching.

26

We research for another hour or more, but after scouring all the old newspapers and even town maps on the computers, we don't find anything of use. Max is right—it feels like all record of the Robertsons and what they did (and what happened to them) was destroyed. Wiped out of the town's history, as if the town wanted nothing more than to forget the tragedy.

I can relate.

"Come on," Max finally says. "Maybe we can bike around town and look for clues. Or try finding the tombstones again. This is a dead end."

I wish he wouldn't use that phrase.

I don't want to leave, though. Even though the ghost was here. Even though she was getting closer. It feels like leaving is giving up.

"Maybe we should go over everything again," I suggest. "Or you can go, and I'll stay."

Max puts his hand on my shoulder. "Come on, man. We're not going to leave you in here. We need some fresh air. And lunch."

My stomach growls at the suggestion.

"Fine," I relent. "But if we don't find anything, we're coming back and researching until we do. At least, I am."

He nods in agreement, and we log out of the computers. Defeated, the three of us leave the library.

I feel it when I'm a few steps out the library door.

The chills on the back of my neck.

The unmistakable feeling of being watched.

I turn.

And there she floats.

Just outside the library door.

I don't look away. Can't look away.

But I do grab wildly behind me, latching onto Lela's arm.

"What?" she asks.

I point with my free hand, straight at the ghost girl.

"There," I whisper. As though I'm afraid of scaring the ghost off, like it's a bird. Which is silly, because I'd like nothing more than for the ghost to go away. "The ghost. Do you see her?"

"I don't see anything," Lela says. She takes a step forward, but I hold her back.

I can't help it. I blink.

And when my eyes open again, her arm is raised and pointed.

Straight.

Back.

At.

Me.

"You're next," I hear her whisper in my ears.

Then, with another reluctant blink, she's gone.

I let go of Lela's arm and drop my free hand. Adrenaline courses through my veins. Adrenaline, and fear.

"Did you hear it?" I ask. Lela shakes her head no.

It's only then that I realize Max is still behind us.

I turn and look back at him. He stands just to

my side, a few feet away, and his eyes are wide with shock.

"Max?" I ask. "Max?"

I go up to him and take his arms, try to get him to focus. He jerks when I touch him, and when his eyes finally lose their glaze and look at me, they water with tears.

"What's wrong?" I ask. Lela stands beside me, looking at him with concern clear on her face.

"I saw her," Max whispers. "I *heard* her."

He takes a deep, shaky breath.

"I'm not sure she was only talking to you," he says. "I think she's also coming for me."

21

Max doesn't want to stay over after that.

I can't blame him. Even though I want to fight for him to stay, even though I don't want to spend another night alone in my house—because I have a horrible feeling that it will be my last—I don't speak up. If roles were reversed, I'd want to be as far away from me and my house as possible.

Heck, I wish I could join him.

Lela and I both offer to walk him home, but he shakes his head.

"I'm fine," he insists.

"You don't look fine," Lela says. "You look like you're about to pass out."

It's true. All the happiness has leached from his face, and his hands shake so hard it looks like he's out in the middle of a snowstorm.

He opens his mouth, probably to refuse again, but Lela won't take no for an answer.

"Come on," she says, walking her bike. "We're taking you home."

"No," he says. His voice is quiet. He looks at me timidly, then looks aside. As if he's ashamed. "I'm sorry, Tamal. Nothing against you. I just . . . I think I'd feel safer if you didn't come. The ghost . . ."

He trails off, shivering so hard he almost collapses, and probably would have if Lela wasn't steadying him. I know what he would have said:

The ghost is only coming after me because of you.

The ghost only found me because we became friends.

Guilt spears my heart, makes it hard to breathe, but I force myself to nod understandingly.

"It's okay. You two go. Max, I can bring your

things to school on Monday. And I'll, um, I'll text you both tomorrow."

He nods and starts to go. Lela looks over her shoulder at me. She seems apologetic, but I bet she's thinking the same thing as Max—this is all my fault.

I watch them walk down the street. When they turn the corner, I call my dad and ask for him to pick me up.

Then I stand there, waiting, alone. Minutes crawl by. Every time I see something from the corner of my eye, I jolt and look over, but it's only ever squirrels or leaves or normal pedestrians. I swear the people walking past look at me funny. As if they know I live in the house on the hill. As if they know I'm the reason the ghost has come back to haunt everyone.

It's only when my dad pulls up to take me back to our cursed house that I realize why standing there had felt so wrong.

I had been alone.

Defenseless.

The perfect time for the ghost to come and take me.

And she never showed.

22

"What's eating you, champ?"

I look over to Dad, who keeps both hands on the wheel but glances at me from the corner of his eye.

"Did you guys get into a fight or something?"

He had clearly been surprised to see that he was only picking me up from town. But he hadn't asked anything until we were in the car and halfway up the hill.

"No," I say, staring out at the trees. "They just, um, they realized that they had plans already."

The lie is flimsy, but he doesn't press for the truth.

"Oh," he says instead. "I'm sorry to hear that." His face brightens. "I guess that just means we'll have to have our own party tonight. Maybe we can break out the ghost-hunting kit."

My blood chills. What's the point of a ghost-hunting kit when the ghost is hunting *you*?

"Yeah," I say, terror racing through my veins. "That would be fun."

As our house comes into view through the arch of trees, I fold in on myself even more. I don't want to come back here. But there's also no safe place to go.

I want to tell him. Honestly, I almost do. *I'm seeing a ghost and Max saw it, too, and if the stories are true, that means the ghost is going to take us, and I'll never see you or Mom again.*

But I don't say that. Because even though he likes watching shows about ghosts and scary things, I don't think he actually believes in them. He likes finding out the rational explanation behind them. And there's no rational explanation behind this.

He sighs when he parks the car in front of the door. When he turns off the engine, though, he doesn't step out.

"Moving is hard," he says, looking at me. His voice has become comforting, his "dad tone." "Big changes like this are always rough. It's normal to miss your old home and friends. Just as it's normal to be angry with me or your mom for bringing you here."

"It's not that," I say. The last thing I want is for him to start thinking I'm angry at them. Then they might think I ran away when the ghost does eventually catch up to me.

"I'm listening."

I swallow and look out the window. Watch the shadows dancing in the woods beyond our house.

"It's the ghost stories," I admit.

I don't know what makes me say it. Maybe I'm hoping that it will feel like when I told Max. That I'll have another person on my side. An adult who believes me. I refuse to tell Dad what I've seen, but there's no harm in admitting something is scaring me. Right?

"I thought as much," he says. He reaches over and puts a hand on my shoulder. "Listen, Tamal. I know I watch a lot of weird stuff, and we talk a lot about creepy things. But they're just stories. The ones your friends told—all places have stories like that. Most small towns have a natural aversion to newcomers, especially ones who come in and try to change things. Stories like the ones Lela told are created to scare new people off. They're old stories, and there aren't any real hauntings. You can't let tall tales get under your skin."

He gets out of the car and I follow suit.

Just like that, I feel the door between us slam shut.

He doesn't believe me. He's already found the rational explanation.

The problem is, the rational explanation doesn't *actually* explain anything.

Especially because, when the shadows shift, I see her in the woods. The ghost girl in the dress. Only this time, she's not facing me. She's facing away . . . facing the town . . . Then I blink, and she is no longer there.

My heart thuds in my throat. I can't speak.

"Come on," Dad says, heading to the house. "We won't talk about ghosts anymore today. I won't even try to find the box with my ghost-hunting stuff. Promise."

Dad pauses halfway to the door.

"Is that why your buddy decided not to stay? He was scared?"

I nod. Then I glance back over my shoulder to the spot where I saw the ghost. She is nowhere to be seen. What was that about? Why was she facing away?

Then things click, and a new terror builds in my chest.

She wasn't pointing at me earlier.

She wasn't avoiding me downtown because she forgot about me.

She had been pointing at Max.

She was coming for him first.

23

I call Max the moment I'm in my room. His cell buzzes a few times.

"Come on," I whisper to the ringing sound. "Pick up pick up pick *up*."

"Hello?" he finally asks.

"You're there!" I reply.

"Course I am," he says. "Why wouldn't I be?"

I flop down on my bed and stare out the window, relief flooding me even as confusion muddles my head. How do I tell him he's in danger without freaking him out? How do I help without making it worse?

"Have you . . . have you seen her again?" I ask. My voice trembles when I say it. I think I might be more scared for him than I was for me.

He doesn't answer right away.

That makes me think the worst.

"No," he finally says. His voice is gruff.

"Good," I say. "Because—"

"I don't want to talk about it anymore," he says. "Lela and I were talking on the way back, and I think she's right. It was just a stupid ghost story, and we were just freaking ourselves out. There's nothing to get worked up over."

"But you saw—"

"I don't know what I saw," he says. "Maybe my eyes were playing tricks on me. Maybe it was a glare from the glass doors."

"But I thought you said—"

"I said I don't want to talk about it anymore," he says. "There's no such thing as ghosts, Tamal. We all need to accept that and grow up. I'll see you Monday."

Then he hangs up, and the phone goes dead.

I stare out into space for a moment, dread sinking in my stomach.

He no longer believes me either.

But I believe—no, I *know*—that he's in terrible danger.

And if he won't listen to me, there's nothing I can do to help him.

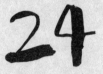

24

I don't stop thinking about Max for the rest of the day. My parents try their best to distract me, which sadly just means doing housework. But even while helping put together new shelves or arranging furniture in the living room or organizing the spice rack, all I can think of is Max and the danger he might be in.

I've texted Lela a dozen times. She, at least, was responsive.

I'm worried about Max, I said.

He'll be okay. He's just scared.

Are you scared?

Not really. I still haven't seen her. Yet.
I hope you don't. She's terrible.

I do. I want proof that she's real.

The admission hurts. If she wants proof, that means she doesn't fully believe me. I'd thought that maybe she had been telling him it was all stories just to make him feel better. But maybe she'd been telling her truth.

Can you keep checking in with him? He doesn't want to talk to me.

Sure. But he'll be okay.

A few minutes pass before she texts again.

If I see the ghost, I'll say hello for you.

It doesn't make me feel any better. She thinks this is a game. A joke. She doesn't understand the danger. Neither of them does. So I try to focus on getting the house in order with my parents. Try to push aside worries of ghosts and hauntings.

It doesn't work.

All I can wonder is if Max is okay.

If he was telling the truth.

If he's seen the ghost again, and if she's getting closer.

I'm so distracted that I drop one of Mom's teacups

as she puts dishes away. I watch it fall to the ground as if in slow motion. It shatters against the linoleum floor. All I can do is stare at the pieces for a while, as if entranced.

"Careful!" Mom says. She hurries over and grabs a broom, then tiptoes across the kitchen and starts sweeping it up. I take a half step back when my bare foot crunches against a piece of ceramic. Pain shoots up my leg and I yelp out.

"Oh, honey," Mom coos. She brushes the pile of ceramic shards away and kneels down beside me. "Let me see."

I lift up my heel.

"Not so bad," she says. "Just a little cut. Arthur!" The last word is a yell. Moments later, Dad pops into the room.

"What is it, dear?" he asks.

"Can you grab the bandages? Tamal cut himself." Dad nods and bounds off.

A minute later, the cut on the back of my heel has been washed and dried and bandaged, and Dad helps me hobble upstairs.

"Why don't you just hang out in your bedroom

for a while?" he suggests. "Try not to put any weight on your foot."

I nod. My foot throbs a little bit, and I feel bad for dropping Mom's teacup. Could this day get any worse?

Actually, scratch that—I already know the answer.

Dad leaves me in my room, where I stare around and wonder what to do with myself. I mean, I know exactly what I should be doing. I should be unpacking. Stacks of boxes line one wall, and the only things out are my bed and a few toys. I make my way over to the boxes and open the lid on the first. Clothes. These, at least, I can't drop and break.

Trying not to put any weight on my foot, I drag the box over to my closet. The closet is honestly the same size as my last bedroom. I can step inside and reach my arms out to the sides and not touch the walls. I reach up and pull the cord on the hanging light. It turns on, flickering slightly.

I do my best to focus on putting clothes away and not worry about Max or the ghost. It's difficult. Every time I move, I swear I see something from the corner of my eye. But it's not the ghost. It's never the ghost. Just shadows and flickering light.

For some reason, the lack of the spirit makes me feel worse.

I'm just about to hang my last shirt when the light above fizzles. There's a small pop, and the light goes out, throwing me into darkness.

Panic floods me; I hadn't realized the closet door had closed behind me, and I stumble around, grasping out and trying to find the handle.

My hand thumps into the wall.

Something else thumps out.

I yelp, my mind racing with images of dead rats or skulls, and moments later, my other hand latches onto the closet doorknob. I yank the door open and look back inside.

There, on the ground, tumbled out of a hidden panel in the wall, lies an old leather journal.

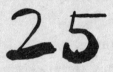

25

My breath catches in my throat.

The journal tumbled out of a secret compartment in the wall. Who hid it there, and why? Whose was it? Instantly, my mind jumps to the ghost girl. But it couldn't be, could it?

I consider calling out to my parents. This could be a trap. Some sort of horrible trick. Maybe if I touch it I disappear. Maybe it holds a terrible curse. I turn away, fully prepared to run downstairs, when another thought passes through my mind.

I've been looking all day for answers, for some clue about the people who lived here and what truly happened to them.

Maybe this is that clue.

If this is the only option available, I have to take it. Even if there's a chance it won't help, or will actually trigger something bad.

My fingers trembling, I reach down and grab the journal, then flop back against my bed. The leather is old and crackles as I open it. The pages are unlined and filled with writing. I carefully skim through the entries, as the pages are just as brittle as the cover. They're all in the same handwriting, all from the same writer. All from the same year.

About a hundred years ago. The same time the house was built.

I know then that I'm holding the ghost girl's journal. It feels forbidden, in a way, and a part of me thinks I should return it to the wall. The rest of me doesn't want to disappear and worries that this may be the only way to prevent that from happening.

Before I can think better of it, I sit back and begin to read.

26

March 23rd, 1919

I'm so bored out here.

Mother and Father won't let me leave the house. They say I'm not to go into town. They say we aren't welcome. They say it isn't safe.

I wish we could go back to the city. At least there I had friends.

At least there I didn't feel trapped.

I don't expect my older brothers, Sam and Elijah, to play with me, but even little Theodore has taken to ignoring me. He has made imaginary friends, and he finds them to be better company. It's just me and Ms. Bear.

I never realized how small a house with so many rooms could feel.

April 3rd, 1919

I do not want to write it. It is too terrible.

Theodore died last night.

He fell down the basement steps. That is what my parents say. That he was wandering the house at night, and he fell down the stairs. But how? He was only three. He would never have walked to the basement.

Was he looking for something?

April 11th, 1919

I miss Theodore with all my heart.

Perhaps that is why I hear him laughing at night.

From the basement. As if he is playing games. As if he is waiting for me to play as well.

It must be that. My imagination.

That must explain why I hear other laughing voices as well.

April 12th, 1919

Mother is sick.

Father says she is making it up. He says it is so we will move back to our old home. I have not seen her since Theodore died. She stays in her room all day and all night. Sometimes I hear her crying.

I miss her.

I miss so many things.

April 29th, 1919

It is my birthday today.

Father forgot. Or perhaps he remembered and did not care. He has not returned from the mill in ages. Mother has not left her room. I worry I will never see either of them again.

I've taken to playing games with Sam and Elijah. They often don't wish to play with me. But today they did. I think they felt sorry for me, or perhaps they are lonely after Theodore's passing as well. It matters not. I am grateful to have friends again.

We played chess. And when that became boring, we played hide-and-seek.

While playing, the most curious thing happened. It was my turn to hide. I snuck down into the basement. Father says we are not to go down there after Theodore fell, but I knew that Samuel and Elijah would never find me there. They would be too scared to venture down.

But someone did. I heard voices down there. I am not certain whose.

I wasn't scared. I heard the voices of other children. They wished for me to play.

I couldn't, of course, because I was already playing with my brothers. But I promised I would come back. I promised we would be friends.

I promised, because one of them sounded exactly like Theodore.

May 15th, 1919

There are so many children here.

So many friends. Even my brother is among them. Even he is able to play.

We play games every day. Though they refuse to leave the basement.

Sam and Elijah think I am lying. They think I

am lying like Mother. She has told me that she hears them, too. Children in the basement. Calling. Sometimes she cries out Theodore's name. I know Theodore misses her. He has told me as much.

Father does not like us to speak of what we hear.

He comes home only rarely. When he returns, my friends and Theodore leave. They do not like him.

I almost prefer it when he is away.

When he is gone, I have my friends. I have my brother back.

And I have heard another voice. A kindly old man. He says I can join them.

He says there is a way.

May 23rd, 1919

Mother died today.

May 26th, 1919

I know she is gone, but sometimes, I hear her.

I hear her, but I do not hear my friends. They have all gone silent. Even Theodore. Perhaps they mourn her. Perhaps they are silent because she could not join them. But I can. I just have to find them again.

Father has stayed home since the funeral. And so, my friends do not return. I miss them.

I will find them.

June 13th, 1919

I cannot eat.

I cannot sleep.

I am so lonely my heart aches.

I wander the halls nightly, holding Ms. Bear.

I miss my youngest brother. I miss my friends. Even my eldest brothers refuse to play. They think I am cursed. Perhaps they are right. Why else would everyone abandon me?

Sometimes I hear the old man. He says that if I help him, I can join them. But I do not trust him. The other children flee when he nears. Just as they flee my father.

So I will search for them on my own.

I will find them.

I must.

I must.

27

I flip back and forth through the pages.

There are more at the beginning, more entries about feeling sad and lonely. But there are no more entries after June 13.

I set down the journal and stare out at the setting sun. How long have I been reading? There's no way it could already be evening. And yet the sky is dark and the scent of dinner is already wafting its way upstairs. Smells like pizza. But even that isn't enough to make me want to leave this room.

My mind races.

The poor girl.

I don't even know her name, but I know how she feels. I've only been here a few days and I already understand the isolation. When Max and Lela aren't around, the place feels far too massive to be comfortable. Even with them, the house still feels empty. I couldn't imagine being locked up in this big house with no friends and no one to play with.

Except . . .

What did she mean about there being so many children here?

What happened to her mother and brothers?

What happened to *her*?

I have more questions now than I did before opening the journal, but before I can read through her entries again or go search for more clues hidden in the closet, Mom calls out from downstairs, making me jump.

"Dinnertime!"

I hide the journal under my bed and go downstairs.

I fully expect the ghost girl to be watching me in the hallway. Especially after reading through her secret diary.

The fact that she isn't puts me on edge.

I don't see the ghost all through dinner.

I don't see her when I run back up to my room and scour the closet for more clues. Not that there are any to be found. The only things she left behind are the journal and a thousand question marks.

When I've brushed my teeth and turned out the light, I have to force myself not to text Max and make sure he's okay. I don't want to scare him any more than I already have.

He can't be a target.

He doesn't live here.

I text Lela instead. She said she'd stay in touch with him.

Is Max ok?

I stare at the chat screen for a long while. She doesn't respond immediately. Or a minute later. Or five minutes later.

It's nearly ten. She can't be asleep already, and I can't imagine there's any other reason she'd have her phone off. Which just makes me come to the very unhappy conclusion: She's ignoring me. Max convinced her I was bad news, that she should stay away from me.

I can't help but feel exactly like I did in New York. But somehow even worse.

There, I *never* had real friends. But here, I'd thought I'd had a chance at that. The ghost was terrifying, sure, but for a brief moment today, we'd been bonded together in seeking an answer. Maybe I was wrong. Maybe they were just trying to use me to see the house, to have a cool story happen to them in a boring town. Maybe everything had been a trick to scare me. Maybe they didn't want me here either. Just like the townsfolk hadn't wanted the original owners.

Maybe they had made up the graveyard to scare the Robertsons off. Maybe they did something terrible to the Robertsons' kids.

Maybe it was all just a cruel game, handed down through the generations. I don't want to believe it, but the longer I lie there, being ignored by the only two kids I thought I could talk to, the more likely the situation feels.

I lie awake for the longest time, staring at the ceiling. I can just imagine Max and Lela telling all their other, *real* friends about tricking me today. Max pretending to see the ghost just so he had an excuse to leave. Lela playing along.

I'll have to go to school alone again. Hang out at lunch and recess alone again. All because I was a joke, and Max and Lela had grown bored of it. Maybe even the ghost was some trick of theirs, some illusion they planted, or a little girl pretending to be a ghost. It would sure explain why there wasn't any written history of the graveyard.

Hours stretch on. I hear my parents go to bed. I hear the creaking of the old house settling, the wind gusting outside.

And then I hear a giggle.

But not the ghost girl's giggle.

It sounds like a little boy, laughing from outside my closed door.

I don't know what makes me do it.

It's like my feet have minds of their own.

I throw back the covers and get out of bed, making my way to the door.

When I open it, no one is there.

But I still hear the laughter. Innocent and child-like. Inviting. Like hearing kids having fun on the playground. I want to be having fun. I want to have friends.

Down the hall. Down the stairs.

My feet lead me there.

I feel like I'm sleepwalking as I make my way to the basement. A small, rational part of me says not to do this, but the rest isn't listening. The rest is sound asleep. And that small, rational voice is screaming to wake up.

My hand reaches for the doorknob.

My fingers close around the cold metal.

The giggling is louder here. And I swear I can hear voices, too, voices calling me down to play, voices I almost recognize . . .

I turn the handle

and a hand clamps down on my shoulder.

29

"Tamal?"

I jerk around to see my dad standing beside me in a robe and slippers.

"What are you doing? Why were you going into the basement?"

It's only then that I realize I'm still clutching the doorknob. I release it quickly, as if afraid it will electrocute me. I can't hear the kids giggling anymore. I can't hear much of anything beyond the humming fridge and my dad's concerned voice.

"I, er . . ."

"Were you sleepwalking?" he asks.

I nod. Even though I've never sleepwalked in my life. Even though I was definitely awake for what just happened.

"Come on," he says. "Let's get you back into bed."

With his hand still on my shoulder, he guides me back up to my room. Now that I'm fully conscious, I realize my foot throbs slightly with every step.

"I used to sleepwalk all the time as a kid," Dad admits. "I'd end up in the kitchen, or on the front yard. I still do at times." He looks down at me and winks. "At least, that's what I tell your mother when she finds me stealing midnight snacks from the fridge."

I know he's trying to make me feel better, and I'm grateful he wasn't filling the silence with some sort of ghost story, but it doesn't calm the fear in my veins. I had been drawn to the basement. Just as Theodore had been. Same as the ghost girl.

What would I have discovered if I went down there?

"Try to get some sleep," Dad says when we reach my room.

I don't ask him what he was doing up in the middle of the night. I don't ask how he found me. I just nod and curl over in bed and close my eyes. When the door shuts behind him, I hide my head under the covers, as if it might be safe under here.

I squeeze my eyes shut and try to force out the echo of what I heard.

The kids' voices, calling me. Asking me to join them. To play.

I swear that one of them sounded like Max.

30

When I wake up Sunday morning, I have a sick feeling in my gut. Maybe because I didn't sleep or maybe because I dread what I have to do. And that is call Max to see if he's okay. The moment my eyes open, I grab my phone from the nightstand and dial. I don't even check to see what time it is—all I know is that the sun is shining, and I don't have any new texts or voice mails, and it already feels like I'm too late.

The phone rings.

And rings.

And rings.

Before going to voice mail.

"*Hey, it's Max, leave a message.*"

I hang up. Because what am I going to say? *Hey, just checking to make sure you weren't taken by a ghost, though if you were I guess you wouldn't get this anyway, and also hopefully you aren't just pretending to be my friend and making all this up to scare me because I swear I heard voices in the basement last night and I don't know what to do. LOL.*

Instead, I send him a text: *what's up?*

Simple. If he answers—whatever he answers—he's okay. If not, he's either taken or ignoring me. Like Lela apparently is.

I flop back in bed and wait.

It's eight. He should be up by now. But maybe he sleeps in on Sundays. Maybe he's watching cartoons. Maybe he and his parents are out. Or maybe, yes, maybe he's proving that it was all just a prank.

After thirty minutes of staring at the ceiling and passing in and out of sleep, I finally roll over and get out of bed. I make my way to the door, wondering if my dad is going to say anything about me sleepwalking the night before. I'm just about to head down the hall when I feel it. Eyes on the back of my neck.

I turn and look behind me.

There, only ten feet away now, is the ghost girl. I stumble back against the door, losing sight of her momentarily.

She is another inch closer.

I run.

31

I can barely eat any cereal I'm so nervous. Not only about the ghost that's now closer than ever before, but because an hour has passed since I reached out to Max and I still haven't gotten a response. Thankfully, Dad doesn't say anything about my sleepwalking, and after a few minutes, I'm free theoretically to do my homework. In practice, I call Max again.

And after a dozen rings, I go straight to voice mail.

I call Lela after.

"Hey," she says. Her voice is confused. Probably because no one calls anymore, let alone before ten a.m. I don't ask why she never responded to my text. That's not as important. At least she's answering now.

"Hey, um. Have you heard from Max today?"

"No, why?"

"Because he's not responding. I've tried a couple times but—"

"Maybe he doesn't want to talk to you."

Her words are a punch to the chest.

"What? Why?"

"Because he's scared," she says. I can practically hear her roll her eyes as she says it. "He always believed the ghost stories more than I did. And now you've got him convinced that he's the next victim."

"But what if he is?"

She sighs heavily.

"They're just scary stories," Lela says.

"I thought you believed in them."

"I don't," she says flatly. "I just think they're fun. Until they're not. I mean, it was great thinking this was a mystery to solve, and getting to explore your creepy house, but Max is really scared. He really thought he saw something yesterday."

That's because he did, I want to say. But I don't, because I worry that would make her hang up.

"I didn't mean for him to get scared," I say.

Another emotion has been creeping into the entire conversation, one stronger and more sinister than fear.

Isolation.

Lela doesn't believe me. Max is scared of me. I want to yell at her and say it's their fault in the first place for telling me these stories, but I know it's not true.

The ghost was always there.

If it's anyone's fault, it's mine for getting them involved.

"Listen," she says. "I'll head over to Max's and make sure he's okay."

"Thanks," I say.

Then she hangs up on me.

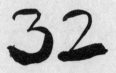

32

I feel the ghost's eyes following me the rest of the morning.

As I rake leaves in the front yard.

As I help Mom move furniture in the living room.

As I once more walk the back hedge, trying without luck to find the hidden tombstones.

I feel the ghost's eyes every step of the way.

But I don't see her again.

Just as I don't hear from Lela again.

33

The ghost reappears at lunch.

I feel her before I see her. I swear I can hear her as well, a hushed constant whisper that buzzes in the back of my brain.

I look up from my sandwich.

And there she is.

On the other side of the kitchen table.

Five feet away.

So close, I can see every strand of her hair.

So close, I can almost see the whites of her eyes.

She floats right between my mom and dad, and neither of them notices a thing.

I startle and press back from the table.

"You okay?" Mom asks.

I can't nod or shake my head. I can't speak. The ghost is right there. Right there between them and I can't scream or do anything to get them to run away. If only Dad *had* brought out some of his ghost-hunting instruments. They'd be going wild right now.

The ghost is there. And when I blink, she is inches closer.

"Soon," I hear her say. *"Soon you will join me."*

"I think he needs a cookie," Dad says. And he smiles broadly, standing up and heading to the sink.

He passes through the ghost girl without even seeing her. He shivers when he passes through.

"Hmm," he mutters to Mom. "We might need to check the windows. I think there's a draft."

The moment he walks through the ghost, she's gone.

But the fear struck through my heart lingers.

34

After lunch, I decide I can't just wait around for something bad to happen. I consider biking into town to find Max and Lela, but since I don't know where either of them lives and I don't want to text them any more than I already have, I know that it would just be a waste of time. There's no point going back to the library, and there's no point trying to research online anymore. There doesn't seem to be much point in anything. All I can do is wait for the ghost to get me, but I don't like that idea at all.

I sit up in my bedroom and pore through the girl's journal one more time, trying to find some clue. Anything.

I keep coming back to *Children in the basement.
Calling.*

Maybe there are more clues down there.

Maybe there's an answer.

"That is mine," a voice whispers.

Right.

Behind.

My ear.

I throw the book down and leap up. But it's not the ghost.

It's Lela.

"What are you—? How did you—?" I gasp. I clutch my chest and feel my heart pounding so hard I swear it will break through my ribs.

I expect her to burst into laughter at my fright, but she doesn't. She looks deadly serious.

"Your parents let me in," she says. She looks down at her feet. "I was going to call you, but I didn't know what to say. Have you . . . have you heard from Max?"

"No," I say, confused. "I thought you were looking for him."

"I was," she says. "I went to his house, and he wasn't there. His parents think he left this morning to hang with you . . ." Her eyes flicker to me. "I need you to swear to me that this isn't a prank, Tamal."

"What?"

She reaches into her pocket and pulls out a phone. Max's phone.

She punches in his passcode—I don't ask how she knows it—and holds it up to me.

To the text conversation between Max and me.

Only . . .

"I never wrote that," I whisper.

"You're telling me the truth?" she asks. She doesn't drop the phone.

"I swear it," I say. I look at her. "What in the world is going on?"

"I don't know," she says. "But I think this is where we're going to find out."

The last text in the thread is from me—a message I know I never wrote or sent.

I found out how to defeat her.

Meet me at the mill.

Tonight.

35

I look at the thread a dozen more times.

"His parents haven't seen him since last night," she says. "They thought maybe he woke up early and was hanging out with us. I told them he was, and that he needed something from his room, which was how they let me in. I don't know if they really believed it, but I didn't want them to worry."

Dread fills me.

"We need to find him," I say.

"No duh," she replies. "That's why I came to find you. We'll go to the mill and look around. Maybe he just went there and got lost or sprained an ankle or something."

I can tell from her voice that she doesn't believe it any more than I do.

"Shouldn't we tell someone?" I ask. "Our parents or the cops or something?"

"Do you think they'd believe us? Besides, he has a text from you. It's suspicious."

I look at the phone again. Why didn't he bring it with him? Had he somehow forgotten it? Or had the ghost actually taken him before he had a chance to leave the house?

"But I was at home," I say. "My parents could vouch for me."

Except . . . would they? After Dad caught me sleepwalking, maybe they would be likely to believe I'd sleeptexted, too. And then—what? I snuck out and captured Max and hid him somewhere?

She raises an eyebrow. That's all she has to do.

"Okay," I say. "I'll get my bike."

I head to the shed near the side of the house. The shed is old and wooden and filled with spiderwebs and gardening tools. It's probably my least favorite place besides the basement, but since the house doesn't have a garage, it's the only place my bike can go.

When I unlock the bike and turn around, she is there.

Hovering in the door.

Four feet away.

"*I just want to play,*" she whispers in my skull. "*I just want to play with you. All of you. Forever.*"

She hovers a few inches closer.

I step back.

And trip over a rake, bringing the bike and a half-dozen garden tools clanging around me.

By the time I scramble back to standing, the ghost girl is gone. Replaced by Lela, who looks at me with a curious expression on her face.

"You okay?" she asks.

I nod.

I'm not, though. The ghost was close. So close. She could almost reach out and touch me.

I don't have much time left.

"Let's go," I say.

Because I know that Max doesn't have much time left either.

If he has any at all.

36

We don't speak as we race toward the mill. Partly because I haven't really biked much and I have to focus on not falling over or tipping into a ditch, and partly because I don't know what to say. I know Lela doesn't believe me, and I know she's more focused on finding Max than worrying about ghosts. I want to tell her about the journal, but that wouldn't prove anything. All it would prove is that I have more material for making up stories.

The mill sits along the river that wends its way through town. At least, what's left of the mill sits there. What was once a massive building is reduced to char and rubble. It stretches along the river, all brick and burnt wood, three stories tall and imposing and very, very empty. I can see the other side of the river through the huge shattered windows and missing doors. One half of the mill is collapsed, and great pillars stick out from the rubble like bones. Even in the light of day, the place feels cold and shadowy. I want to go in there even less than I want to hang out in our shed.

We stop in front of it. There's no easy entrance. Everything is covered in weeds and brick and rusted pipes. It practically screams *tetanus*, but Lela isn't dissuaded. She drops her bike against a large pile of bricks and begins pacing, trying to find an entrance through the debris. I park as well and begin poking around, walking the other direction, as the mill stretches for blocks and Max could be anywhere. Even though I can see through the building, I can't see anyone in the shadowy interior.

I try to stick to the sunny patches.

Every once in a while, from the corner of my eye, a shadow looks an awful lot like the ghost girl.

"Max!" I call out. "Max, are you in there?"

My voice echoes through the cavernous ruins of the mill. Nothing moves.

I walk a bit farther along the edge of the ruins and find a small blackened path through the debris. I glance behind me; Lela is near the far end, I can just make out the top of her head over the piles of rubble. For a moment, I consider calling out to her, but then I hear laughter farther in.

It sounds like Max.

Carefully, I make my way down the rock-strewn path, through arched and burnt timbers, into the heart of the ruined mill.

It's much colder inside, and dark shadows stretch over everything, making it impossible to see even in the middle of the afternoon.

But I don't need to see, not really. I can hear Max now, laughing and talking. I can hear other kids as well, all giggling. It sounds like they're playing. But I know that there isn't anyone here; I would have seen them from outside.

Right?

"Max?" I call out.

More laughter, but no real response. Chills race

up and down my arms as I creep closer to where I hear the voices. I pick my way over the stone and fallen wood carefully, the rushing sound of the river growing louder. A voice in the back of my mind says that this is dangerous, that the mill could fall apart at any moment. There isn't even any graffiti in here, as though even the vandals know to keep out. So what am I doing here?

Up ahead is a giant concrete wall.

Against it leans a bicycle.

Max's bicycle.

The kids' laughter is coming from behind there.

Max is behind there.

I know he is.

I quicken my pace. Rocks scatter as I rush. The laughter grows louder with every step. He's here! He's here! He wasn't in danger after all.

I round the corner of the wall.

And when I see not Max but just more empty space, I hear Lela scream.

37

Reality tilts as I realize that Max isn't here at the same moment I know Lela is in danger.

I run.

Through the abandoned, destroyed mill, toward the sound of Lela's yell. She's far away. Too far. I stumble over bricks and burnt toppled pillars, dart around piles of crumbled stone. My breath burns from the dust I kick up and the fear in my heart.

Up ahead, I see her.

She's backed against a wall. Her eyes are wide as she stares at something straight in front of her, something I can't see due to the piles of rubble in the way. Lela screams again.

And that's when I see the ghost girl.

Floating closer to Lela. Only a few feet away. And moving quickly. Far too quickly.

I'm five feet away when Lela looks over.

I'm five feet away when the ghost's outstretched hand is inches from Lela's face.

Lela's eyes are pleading as she looks at me.

As we both realize I'm too far.

Too late.

"Help me," Lela begs.

Then the ghost's finger touches Lela's cheek.

The moment they touch, Lela and the ghost both disappear.

38

I stand in shock. The only sound is the blood hammering in my ears and the distant chatter of birds and the rushing river. The only sight is the dust sifting through beams of light.

Lela's empty footprints in the dirt.

Gone.

Gone.

"Lela!" I yell out. "Lela, where are you?"

My voice is raspy as reality hits me like a brick to the chest.

She's gone.
The ghost took her.
Just as the ghost took Max.
Just as the ghost will take me.

39

I scour the mill for the next twenty minutes. But after poking through every hiding place, one thing becomes terribly clear: Max and Lela aren't here.

Dread fills me. Not just because I know I'm next, but because it's all my fault; soon, Lela's and Max's parents are going to realize their kids aren't coming home, and they'll be devastated.

All I wanted was to make friends, but getting them involved in my life cost them theirs.

I collapse against a pile of rubble, ignoring the pain of stone biting into my back, and start to cry.

It's my fault.

It's all my fault.

I have to find a way to get them back, even though I know there's no getting them back. If the kids in the ghost story could return, there wouldn't have been a ghost story in the first place.

Through the haze of my tears, I see her. Wavering in front of me like a mirage. Only she is definitely not a mirage.

I force myself up to standing and wipe the tears away.

She's only feet away from me.

She could reach out and touch me. Make me disappear like she did to Lela.

A part of me almost wants her to. At least then the nightmare would be over.

But if she does, I can't help my friends. I can't save them.

"Wh-why are you doing this?" I stammer.

I don't expect her to answer.

She tilts her head to the side. I can see a glint of her eyes through the long, gnarled strands of her hair. Is what Max said true—does this mean it's already too late?

"Because I'm lonely. Because I don't want to be alone anymore."

She floats forward.

"Let me try to help you," I say. I sidestep the rubble I'd leaned against, try to make space between us. "I know I can. I found your journal. I know—"

"You read my journal?" she screams.

Her head snaps upright. And I see it then—I see her face.

A little girl's face, but contorted with rage. Her eyes wide and bloodshot, her mouth elongated in a howl, revealing inky blackness.

She wails.

Lunges toward me.

I turn and run.

I don't look back.

40

Mom and Dad call out the moment I'm inside, but I don't respond. I couldn't even if I wanted to—the bike ride up here winded me, but I know I don't have time to rest. I run straight to my room and grab the journal from my bed. I have a plan. It's not much of one, but I don't have time to try and figure out anything else.

When I stand and turn from the bed, she's there.

Floating in the doorway. I can see her face still, and even though it isn't as grotesque as it was before, it's still terrifying. Her eyes are shadowed and narrowed, and her lips pulled down in a frown.

"That's mine," she growls.

There's no way I can get past her if she stays in the door. I don't think. With panic racing in my veins and the clock ticking, all I can do is act.

I throw the journal at her.

It flies straight through her, but she fades the moment it bounces off the wall.

I run, grabbing the journal as I go.

I thud down the stairs, past my parents, and toward the basement.

Every step of the way, the ghost girl follows me. Getting closer.

My hand grabs the basement door handle. When I yank it open and run down the wooden steps, I see her hand reach out, past my shoulder, swiping for me.

And barely missing.

There isn't anyone down in the basement. The door latches shut behind me, casting me into a thick darkness broken only by a flickering overhead light.

My parents hammer on the door, trying to get in.

I know they won't get in.

The ghost wants me.

Just me.

Now that she has my friends, I'm all that's left.

I rush to the center of the basement, the journal clutched to my chest, and turn around wildly.

The ghost flickers in and out of my vision.

Blink, and she's three feet to my left.

Blink, and she's to my right.

Blink, and she's missing.

Until I turn and see her floating only inches behind me.

"Give them back," I say.

Every nerve in me wants to retreat, but I don't. I'm not running from her. Not anymore. This is where she said she heard the voices. The ghosts. The missing children. And this is where it has to end.

The girl tilts her head to the side.

"Give back my friends," I continue. "And I'll let you take me. I'm the one you want. I'm the one who lives here."

She smiles behind her lank hair, her lips cracking.

"*We all live here now*," she says. "*This is our home. Our* real *home. Your friends are all waiting for you.*"

She raises her arms to the sides.

And from the shadows emerge the ghosts.

A dozen small children. All wearing clothes from

different time periods. A boy in a blazer. A girl in a nightgown. Twins in matching shirts. There are older kids, too, high schoolers in fairly modern jeans and T-shirts. And there, farther in the shadows, are Max and Lela, looking at me with sad, blank eyes. There is another shape behind them, his hands on their shoulders: an old man in dusty coveralls, most of his transparent body hidden in shadow.

"*You will join us,*" the ghost girl says. "*Forever.*"

The ghosts close in around me.

And while my parents call out from upstairs and the ghosts gather close, the girl reaches out and touches my forehead, and the world goes white.

41

White.

White and gray and black, the tones shifting and blurring together like ocean waves.

I blink.

The landscape slowly solidifies, until I realize I'm standing in the upstairs hallway.

What am I doing in the hallway?

And why . . .

I look around.

It's definitely the upstairs hallway. Except it's different. Bleak.

That's when I realize what's wrong.

There aren't any colors.

Everything is white and gray and black. I look down at my hands. They're gray as well.

"What in the world?" I whisper.

Fear starts racing through my veins.

I remember the basement.

I remember the ghost.

I remember her touching me.

And then . . . then I was here, in the hall.

I look around. The ghost is nowhere to be seen.

Why is everything gray?

What happened?

Maybe something's wrong with my vision. Maybe I suddenly need glasses or something, from the shock. I mean, I thought the ghost was taking kids away, so what am I still doing in my home?

Then I hear it. Yelling downstairs. My parents, yelling out my name.

"Tamal!" my dad calls out. His voice sounds distant. Like it's coming from the end of a long hallway.

"Tamal, where are you?" Mom echoes.

"Up here!" I call.

"Tamal!" Dad calls out again.

Did he not hear me?

I sigh and head down the hall, thudding heavily down the steps as I walk. I don't know how I'll explain to them why I'm coming from the upstairs hall when they saw me going into the basement. Secret passage?

"I'm right here," I say when I reach my parents.

They stand in front of the basement door. Dad is coming up the basement steps, shaking his head.

"He's not down there," he says.

"Maybe there's an exit we didn't notice before?" Mom asks frantically. "It's an old house. Didn't they have doors for ice delivery or something?"

"All boarded up," Dad says. "He's not down there. I checked everywhere."

"But he can't have just disappeared!"

"Hello?" I call out, waving my hands. I'm only like five feet away, and I'm definitely not mumbling. "I'm right here!"

"I'm *sure* he came down here," Mom says.

"It's been an hour, Nadiya. He's not in the basement. Maybe he went to see his friends."

"Mom? Dad?" I ask. *An hour? I've only been gone a few seconds.*

"I'm going to go check outside," Mom says. "Maybe we missed him."

"Okay. I'll try calling his friends' parents again."

"I'm right here!" I yell out.

But my parents don't seem to notice.

They turn. Look straight at me without seeing me.

And then my mom heads to the front door

   and walks right through me.

42

I stand there, frozen, as my parents leave the hall.

Reality shatters around me. Mom just walked through me as if I wasn't there. Neither of them saw me. And yet I'm here, in the hall, staring at the open basement door. I'm here.

So why did they act like I wasn't here?

How did she walk through me?

I run to an oval mirror hanging on the wall.

I can't see my reflection.

It's as if I'm . . .

As if I'm . . .

"A ghost?"

I turn slowly.

There, a few feet away, stands the ghost girl.

And she is smiling.

43

"What did you do to me?" I ask. My voice wavers. "Am I dead?"

She shrugs. Takes a few steps forward. She's no longer floating, though she still holds the teddy bear in her hand. She doesn't look nearly as terrifying, though the smile makes her look sinister.

"I brought you here," she says. "To play with me. To keep me company."

"But my family—" I say. "They didn't see me. Why didn't they see me?"

Another shrug. Another step toward me. I take a step back.

"You know why they didn't see you," she says.

"Because I'm a ghost." The words drop from my mouth, but I can't believe I spoke them. I don't want to believe them. But now that I've spoken it, a part of me fears it to be true. "You killed me?"

"No," she says. "I brought you here so we could be friends. Didn't you want friends? You were lonely. An outsider. Just like me."

"I had friends," I whisper. I take another step back. I'm close to the basement now, only a step or two away from tumbling back into the darkness. "I had friends, but you took them away."

"No," she repeats. "I didn't take them away. I brought them here. So we could be together. All of us."

She gestures out to the sides, and from the walls and the floor float children. Dozens of children. Young boys and girls, my age or younger. All of them grayscale and translucent. Like me. They stare at me with blank faces and white eyes. I take another step back. Teeter on the edge of the basement stairs.

"We will play forever," she says. "Look, even your friends will join."

Two kids step forward. A little more solid than the others, but no less monochrome.

Lela and Max.

Their eyes stare at me, wide and white, like pearls or moons. They open their mouths, but neither of them speaks. I shudder in fear.

"What did she do to you?" I whisper to them.

"They cannot speak. None of them can," the ghost girl says. "But you . . . you are different. That's why I brought you here."

The ghost girl steps forward.

"My name is Alice," she says. "And we are going to be best friends. Forever."

I take another step back and topple into the basement.

The world tumbles and spins, and then the basement door closes and traps me in darkness.

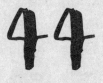

I blink and look around, expecting the ghostly Alice
to appear at any moment to torment me. But she
doesn't. Instead, a moment later, the door opens and
my dad looks down.

"Tamal?" he calls out. "Was that you?"

"Honey," my mom says, "he's not here. We know
he's not here."

"But the door—"

"It was just the wind," she says sadly. The two of
them glance toward the basement once more. They
look straight at me. But their expressions are sad.

"Come on, let's go search the neighborhood. Maybe he got lost."

When she closes the door and sends me back into darkness, I know there's no hope of them ever seeing me.

I run up the stairs anyway. My hand reaches toward the doorknob and passes straight through. I stumble in shock, momentum propelling me forward,
and fall straight through the door.

My parents are already walking toward the front door. I chase after them, yelling at the top of my lungs even though I know it won't work.

Mom and Dad step out.

I step after them
toward the open door
and slam into nothing.

"What?" I ask no one.

I ball my fist and slam it forward, where it smashes against thin air as though an invisible window of steel is stuck in the doorframe.

"You're stuck here," the girl says.

I jump and look over, and there she is, appearing out of nowhere.

"After a while, you get used to it. Not being able to leave. Them not seeing you," she continues. She looks up the stairs, and her expression makes me think that she isn't talking about her own parents. She lowers her voice. "If you're lucky, they'll leave soon. And then you won't have to think about them ever again. Just like they won't think about you ever again."

"My parents wouldn't do that," I say. My lips tremble. "They wouldn't just leave me."

"I thought that, too," she whispers. "But my dad left and my brothers left. They always leave. And then you're here, alone. Only . . ." Her face brightens slightly. "We aren't alone. You're here with me now. And when your parents leave, you'll stay. Forever."

And even though I don't have a body, I feel my stomach fall, already imagining the worst. My parents up and leaving, moving back to New York without me.

I'll stay here with her and watch the next family move in.

Maybe I'll become like the girl and steal other children away. Just to have friends. Just to have someone to talk to and play with. Even just thinking that

makes me feel terrible. I could never do that to someone else.

But after a hundred years . . .

"Why can't I leave?" I ask. "You were able to follow me."

She shrugs.

"I was chosen to help him gather children. No one
else but I can leave. I think it's so I can bring others
back here. But don't worry. You don't have to leave.
All your friends are already here."

. Max and Lela step out from the basement door
then, holding hands and looking at me with sad
expressions. Who is she talking about? Who wants to
gather children? I'm reminded of the ghostly old man
in coveralls I'd seen standing behind Max and Lela.
But before I can ask, Alice continues.

"Play with us," Alice says. Her eyes darken.
Shadows pool above her cheekbones, and her teeth
and gums turn black as her hair rises around her head
in a serpentine halo. "Play with us, or I will make
sure you never play again."

I look around the empty house. Empty, save for
the dozens of ghosts trapped within.

Trapped, just like me.

Then I look to Alice. The one who dragged me here. Away from my family. Away from life.

Alice, who looks like she will happily deliver on her threat.

"Okay," I say in defeat. "Let's play."

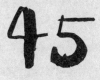

We play the rest of the afternoon.

It is the least fun I've ever had playing games in my life. Er, death. And even though only a few hours pass, it seems to go on forever.

It starts fun enough.

"Let's play hide-and-seek," Alice suggests. Of course, she offers to count first.

The ghosts scatter. They vanish through walls or doorways as Alice stands there, holding her teddy bear, counting out loud. Even Max and Lela disappear into thin air; I want to run after them, to try to talk to them, to try and form a plan together.

I don't want to play games. I want to figure out how to get out of here, how to be alive again. I know there has to be a way. *Has* to. But I'm also acutely aware of how dangerous it would be to upset Alice. So I do what she asks. At least it gives me time to figure out how to get out of this mess.

I immediately run up to my room. The door is closed, but I'm starting to get the hang of being a ghost, and I pass through the wood like it's nothing more than mist.

I'm not alone.

"Lela!" I yelp in surprise. She stands beside my bed, looking around, her expression vacant. I run over to her. "Lela, are you okay?"

She doesn't respond. Just stares at me like I'm a mildly interesting rock or something.

I reach out to touch her, but my hand goes straight through her shoulder.

"Lela," I say, softer. "We have to try to get out of here. We can't be gone for good. If we just work together, if we just think—"

But before I can finish my sentence, her eyes go

wide. She looks over my shoulder, and when I turn to see, she vanishes.

Alice stands in the doorway.

"You're going to have to try harder," she says, staring at me angrily as I stand there in the center of the room. "You're no fun if you're trying to lose. And bad things happen to kids who aren't fun."

"Why are you doing this?" I ask. My ghostly heart is beating hard in my chest—it felt like the old man was watching us. Waiting for me to screw up, or ask the wrong thing. I lower my voice. "Why are you trapping us here? Is it the old man? You wouldn't have wanted this when you were alive. You wanted to escape, too."

She narrows her eyes. I can almost see her fighting herself, her expression angry and confused.

"I have to," she whispers. "He makes me."

Then it's like a gloss comes over her face.

"I have to find the others," she says. "*They* know how to play the game."

She vanishes, leaving me with more questions than answers.

46

We keep playing.

After an hour of hide-and-seek, in which Alice is *always* the seeker and the rest of us are always found within moments, we play games I didn't think kids my age played anymore. Duck, duck, goose and charades, which seems like a strange game to play since none of the other ghosts talk. We're up in one of the empty rooms, overlooking the front drive.

"Oh, this is so much more fun with you around," Alice says. "You can talk."

"Why can't they?" I ask in a whisper as some

unknown boy acts out what looks like a quacking duck. It feels rude to mention it.

She shrugs.

"I'm not quite certain," she replies. "I can talk. A few of the original ghosts can speak, but they don't say much beyond asking to play. I think they've forgotten how to say anything else. But everyone else is silent. Well, except for William. That's okay, though—you're here now, and we'll continue having fun forever."

"Who's William?"

Her expression shifts from delighted to scared. She doesn't answer me, just pushes herself up to standing and announces that it is her turn.

I look around the group; she doesn't have to say who William is. Only one ghost here could scare her like that. The old man in overalls. I wonder what he's doing here, and what he wants from us.

As Alice settles into the next round of boring games, and I start wondering if I'll also lose my mind and will to speak after a century of playing children's games, I hear gravel crunching in the front drive. I push myself from the circle and go over to the window, sadness filling me. I want so badly to rush downstairs, to yell out to them, to give them a hug. My whole body aches with that want, and the knowledge that unless I do something—fast—I'll never feel them hug me again.

They step out of the car in the darkness, and I can tell they're feeling just as bad as I am. Clearly, their search for me and Lela and Max didn't bring them any closer to the truth. My mom walks over and puts her arm over my dad's shoulders. I can tell even from here that he's crying.

It breaks my heart to see them both so sad. To know they think they've failed. When I'm here. I'm right here. But I might as well be an ocean away. I wish I could tell them it's okay, that it's not their fault. I wish I could let them know that I see them. Frustration builds inside me. I want them to know I'm here. I want them to see.

They have to.

They *have* to.

I know there's no point, but I smack my palm against the window.

My dad looks up.

Stares at the window.

His eyebrows furrow. As if he sees . . . maybe not me, but something.

And for the first time since Max was stolen away this morning, I feel a small spark of hope.

47

Ghosts don't sleep.

If I were alive, that would be a fun realization. More time to play video games or hang out with friends or watch TV or even just walk outside. But as a ghost, I can't do any of those things. Not that I don't try.

I stand behind the sofa and watch my parents watch the news. I know they're hoping for some sign of me on there, and the fact that I'm right behind them, while they're hoping against hope for a trace of me on the news, is a stab to the heart.

At one point, my dad starts crying again, and Mom pulls him in for a hug. I reach over and try to comfort him, but my hand goes straight through them both.

Even though my tears don't leave an impression, I cry, too.

Hours later, they go to bed. I don't follow. I sit on the sofa and try multiple times to pick up the remote, but it never works. My hand slides through it like mist. After an hour of staring at nothing, listening to the house settle, I get up and move about. If I sit there any longer, I'll go mad.

In the dark, the halls seem to stretch on forever.

I wander from room to room, everything dim but still somehow lit, as though my ghostly eyes have some sort of night vision. It would be cool if not for the fact that there's nothing for me to do. I wander from room to room, trying to think of a way out, trying to think of something I can do to get my parents' attention.

When I stop by my door and look in, I find Max and Lela inside.

They both hold hands, and they stand in front of the window, looking out. Toward the hill stretched far, far below. To their own homes. The homes I know they'll never see again. Unless we can figure something out.

"I was wondering where you were," I say.

They turn around slowly. Their eyes seem unfocused as they look at me. Honestly, they don't seem to see me any better than my dad did. What in the world is going on?

I step toward them.

"We have to find our way out of here," I continue. "I know there's a way. I think my dad heard me. I think he can help."

Both of their eyes go wide, and their mouths open in a silent scream.

Moments later, they vanish. And even though I'm a ghost, goose bumps crawl over my skin.

"I can see you're going to be a problem," growls a man's voice. I turn to find the man in coveralls standing in the door. He doesn't look happy.

"Do you know what I do with problem children?" he asks.

I shake my head.

He growls again and thunders forward. He grabs my shoulder—hard—and pulls me in close, so I can see all of his broken teeth and gnarled features.

"Then I think it's time you found out. Even the dead can be scared."

48

Blackness crushes me.

I want to scream out, but the air is stuck in my lungs.

Distantly, I hear howling. Like a hundred hungry dogs on the hunt. Like the most terrible storm. Like a thousand lost souls wanting to devour me.

I don't know how, or where, but I run.

The blackness twists and stretches, becomes a windowless hall that carries on for eternity. I run. And behind me the howling gets louder.

It's getting closer.

So much closer.

I don't want to know what will happen when it catches me.

I run faster, and the howling becomes laughter.

"Run faster, little man," the howling cackles roar. "Run faster, or I will *devour* you!"

I look over my shoulder, and there are shapes in the darkness. Bone-white gnashing teeth and fiery-red eyes and ghoulish faces, talons outstretched. I stumble.

I scream.

And the hallway vanishes. Replaced by my room once more, and the builder—William—stands in front of me, a grim, victorious smile on his face.

"I built this house," he says. "And I kept building it, even after I died. I've built horrors you can't even imagine. But if you keep being a problem, you will. I will lock you away in them for eternity."

The stories click.

"You were the builder who died here."

"Bingo. I gave my life for this house. And what did I get? An eternity of torture."

I swallow hard and try not to flinch back. Even in death, his breath smells horrible.

"Why are you doing this?" I ask. "Why won't you just let us go?"

His smile becomes sinister.

"Because if I have to be miserable for eternity, I will bring everyone I can with me. Especially the rotten kids who live here—they're the reason I'm dead. If their parents hadn't wanted a big fancy house, I wouldn't have had to work so quickly. I wouldn't have lost my life. But I did. And I'm trapped. And so, bucko, are you."

He stands and pushes me back. I stumble and try not to fall.

"This is my final warning," he says. "Play by the rules. Or I'll make your afterlife even worse."

With a flash of red eyes, he vanishes.

49

I have to find a way out of here.

I don't know which is worse—being stuck playing boring games or being chased by a nightmare.

I'm so angry at Alice I could scream. She's the reason I'm here in the first place. She's been nabbing kids for William to torture. This is her fault. All of it.

Tears well in the corners of my eyes. The scream builds inside me.

And you know what, why not? It's not like anyone can hear me.

I take a deep breath and scream at the top of my lungs.

It goes on for a long time, because I guess ghosts don't really need to worry about losing their breath. And it feels so, so good. I scream because I'm angry— at Alice, at myself—and I'm frustrated and honestly, terribly scared. I scream because I don't want to imagine my parents moving away and leaving me here. I don't want to imagine being stuck here for eternity.

The door in front of me flies open.

My scream cuts off, and I take a step back as Dad comes into the hall. He looks around, blinking wildly. I swear, for the briefest moment, his eyes actually focus on me before he looks back to the shadows.

"Arthur, what is it?" my mom asks.

"Nothing, Nadiya," he replies. He looks up and down the hall again, then says, quieter, "Just thought I heard something."

Once more, hope bubbles inside me.

Even though he looks right through me now, he heard me.

He heard me, and that feels like the first step toward getting out of this nightmare.

50

I know William the builder is watching me. I can feel his eyes on the back of my neck.

I wander the halls for what feels like hours. I don't see anyone. Not Max or Lela. Not any of the other ghost children.

Not Alice.

I feel more alone than ever before. Even though I know my dad can hear me, I don't know how he could possibly get me out of this. Especially with William watching.

I'll only have one shot at escaping, and I can't blow it.

Alice is the only ghost who's been able to step foot outside of here. The only ghost who seems to have a memory of her former life. She must be the key. She has to have an idea how to escape.

I just have to find her.

And when I finally face my fear and go down into the basement, I do.

She kneels on the floor, crying into her hands and facing away from me.

I walk up to her and place a hand on her shoulder. Strangely, my hand doesn't pass through her like it did Lela, but rests lightly on her shoulder, her skin cold and hard like porcelain. Finally touching something relatively solid is a relief.

It's then that I see what she's kneeling over.

Her journal. It sits exactly where I dropped it when she took me away.

"What's wrong?" I ask.

I don't know why I'm trying to comfort her. Habit, I guess. I want to be angry with her. Want to let her stew and cry down here in the dark on her own. But that anger flickers so quickly it's like it was never there.

Alice is still a kid. Just like me. It's clear that William has her trapped just like the rest of us. Can I really blame her for wanting to bring more kids here? For wanting more friends?

She sniffles and looks up at me, wiping her eyes dry.

"My journal," she says.

"What about it?" I ask.

"I can't pick it up. I can't read it. I can't . . . I can't remember . . ." And she breaks into tears again.

I don't know what compels me. I crouch down on the ground beside her and wrap her in a hug. She collapses against me, sobbing uncontrollably. All I can do is sit there and pat her on the back as her tears puddle dryly on my shoulder.

Finally, she calms herself again and sits back. She doesn't look at me, though. She stares at her closed journal.

"I'm sorry," she says. "It's just . . . You're the first person I've actually been able to talk to in so many years. And when I saw you had my journal . . ." She takes a deep, shuddering breath. "It's been so long. I can barely even remember what happened to me. Who I was before I became this." She holds up her translucent hands. "I hoped maybe I could read my journal again. Try to remember who I was. But I can't even turn the pages."

She reaches down and tries to flip open the cover, but her fingers just pass straight through.

Another tear drops down to the floor, fading instantly.

"I've been so lonely. I've forgotten what my parents looked like. What my brothers looked like. Sometimes I think all I've ever been is a ghost. Sometimes I think the only family I've ever had is the other ghosts." She lowers her voice. "And William."

"He scares me," I admit in a whisper.

"Me, too," she replies. "He scares me more than anything."

"Is that why you do it?" I ask. "Is that why you keep bringing more kids here?"

"He makes me. He says if I don't, he'll make my life a nightmare. But . . . that's not the only reason. I'm lonely. So lonely. No one else can speak to me. No one else can really play. I keep hoping that I'll find someone who could truly be my friend. That's also why I brought the kids here. I guess . . . I guess I'm just as much of a monster as William is."

"You're not," I reply. Even though I'm mad at her, it's clear she's not doing any of this because she's mean or evil. She's lonely. "I know what it's like to be lonely. To wish you had friends. It's the worst. I can understand why you'd want to bring others here."

"It doesn't even matter anymore," she says. "I'm forgetting who I am. Who I was. Sometimes I think I'm just William's puppet."

An idea forms in my mind.

"Maybe I can help," I say. "I . . . I read your journal. What if I told you what I remember reading?"

She looks at me, and her tear-filled eyes fill with hope.

"Would you?"

I nod, and tell her what I can recall.

When I finish telling her what I remember, she actu-
ally smiles. She appears more like a little girl than
ever before. She looks down at the journal and pats
the cover lovingly. Her hand passes right through.

"Thank you," she tells me. "Thank you for helping me remember who I was. I remember now. Most
of it, I think."

"Why do you think you were different?" I ask.

She furrows her eyes.

"After my mother and youngest brother died, I
was very sad, and very lonely. I remember going to the
basement, because I thought I heard Theodore calling

out to me. Only, when I got there, it was William. He said that this was all my fault. He said he was going to take each of us, one by one. But I offered to help him. I said that if he spared the rest of my family, I'd bring him more children. He agreed. My dad and two older brothers left. I never saw them again."

"What about your younger brother, Theodore?" I ask.

Tears form in her eyes. "He isn't here. Neither is my mother. I don't know what happened to them. But I think that that is why I can speak and remember—William let me keep my words and my thoughts so I could help him bring in more kids. It's all my fault. I wish . . . I wish I hadn't brought you into this. But I'm also glad, because without you, I would have forgotten myself entirely. Perhaps now eternity won't be so bad."

The statement makes my heart clench. *Eternity.* I can't wait that long. I refuse.

"It's not your fault. You only did what you were forced to do. And I know that's not true—there has to be a way out," I say. I keep my voice down, for fear that William is listening in.

Alice shakes her head.

"There isn't. I can leave the house only to chase after people who have stepped foot here," she says. "Otherwise, I'm stuck. I can't just walk out the front door. I've tried. I always end up back here. Besides, with William always watching, there's no way we could escape."

"What about the others?" I say. "Why can't they talk? Why am I the only one who seems . . . ?"

"Alive?" she asks. "I don't know. Maybe because you offered yourself up. Everyone else, I had to chase down."

I rack my brains, trying to remember everything I've learned from watching silly ghost shows with Dad, or reading different ghost stories.

"Do you have any unfinished business?" I ask.

"What do you mean?"

"I mean, a lot of times ghosts linger in a place because they're holding a grudge, or because they have a message to share."

She shakes her head. Her eyes well with tears again.

"I just want to leave," she whispers.

I sigh. "What about the other ghosts? The original kids? The ones that lured you down here in the first place. Were they working for William, too?"

"I don't think so," she says. "They were here long before William ever started building. This used to be a graveyard for children, you know. He built right on top of them. I think that's why they're here. The builders tore up their tombstones and threw them in the back woods. That's when everything started going wrong. If anyone has unfinished business, it's them."

The graveyard. That's it. Everyone knows not to build on a cemetery. *Especially* not a children's cemetery. What if the house is cursed because of that? What if, now that the graves are disrupted, no one who dies here is able to escape? What if that's why William is stuck and trying to enact his revenge? I've seen it in countless shows my dad and I watched.

"That's it," I whisper.

"What is?"

"The original grudge. William isn't the driving force—it's the children's graveyard. Your family made William build on a place he shouldn't, and that cursed the house. I think . . . I think that so long as this house stands, we're all cursed to be stuck here."

"So what do we do? We can't exactly tear the house down. I can't even pick up my journal."

"No," I say. I refuse to be defeated. This has to be the answer. *Has* to. "But I know someone who might believe us. I hope."

52

Dad doesn't disappoint.

The next morning, after breakfast, I watch him head up to one of the spare rooms. I follow, hope blossoming in my chest. Sure enough, he goes into the room with all his ghost-hunting equipment. He rummages around in a few boxes, finally pulling out what looks like a strange old tape recorder.

It's supposed to help amplify the voices of ghosts. Which is exactly what I hope it will do.

It never worked before. But I've also never been a ghost with a mission before.

I sent Alice to go distract William. I'm not certain what she'll do or how long it will work, but I'm hoping it's enough to buy us some time.

Dad sets the strange black microphone on a cardboard box and switches it on. A loud static noise fills the room as the device amplifies all the unheard sounds.

"Tamal?" he whispers. "Tamal, are you there?"

"Dad!" I yell. My voice comes through the speaker, muffled and muted through the static, but fairly clear. "Dad, it's me! I'm here!"

Dad cries out in relief.

"Tamal! It's you. I knew I had seen you. What's going on? Where are you?"

"I'm trapped, Dad," I say. Even though I've internally rehearsed this a hundred times since coming up with the plan, my words come out in a confused, frantic jumble. "I don't have much time. The builder of the house is here, and he's trapping kids for eternity. I think it's all because this house was built on a graveyard. And I think—"

Someone roars behind me, so loud it makes the ghost speaker shake and fall off the cardboard box.

I look back.

William.

Except now, he no longer looks human. He is monstrous. Seven feet tall and as wide as a car, with shadows leaching from his eyes and claws sprouting from his fingers.

Alice is nowhere to be seen.

"You thought you could trick me!" William roars. His voice echoes through the ghost speaker that Dad tries to set upright. "You thought I would let you escape?"

"Tamal!" Dad calls. "Tamal, what's happening?"

"I warned you, boy. And now you'll pay!"

The monstrous William, twisted by years of hate and isolation, lunges at me.

But when he's a foot away, his clawed hand outstretched, Alice appears from nowhere and grapples him from behind. Her arms go around his neck. He roars in anger.

"Quickly, Tamal, quickly!" she yells.

I look to my dad, whose eyes are wide with fear and confusion and—I think—helplessness.

"Dad, you're the only hope. The house is cursed. It was built on a children's cemetery."

Behind me, Alice holds on for dear life, and William thunders around trying to pull her off his back.

"You have to tear down the house, Dad. Get Mom out of here and tear it down. It's the only way. It's the only—"

"Tamal!" Alice yells. I look at her. "Tamal, he's too strong. I'm going to try to trap him in the nightmare he built, but you have to work fast. For me. For all of us."

My eyes widen as William roars.

As shadows seep out from the sides of the room.

They twist around William and Alice. Cocoon them in darkness.

William howls again, wolflike and defeated.

"Thank you," Alice calls out. "Thank you for helping me remember."

And then, in a twist of shadow, the two of them are gone.

Panic races in my chest. I look back to my dad.

"We don't have much time, and I don't know if it will work, but it's the only way," I say. Tears choke in my throat. "Just know . . . I love you, Dad. Both of you."

"I love you, too, Tamal," Dad says. He holds out his hand. It wavers in midair. I take it. I don't know if he feels it.

We stare at each other for a moment.

Then the house rumbles, as if in an earthquake. Dad topples to the side.

The ghost box clicks off.

In the distance, in the nightmare, I hear William roar in anger as he tries to break free. As the entire house shakes with his fury.

Dad doesn't waste any time. He grabs some things and runs downstairs.

I run, too. And hope that wherever I go, William can't follow.

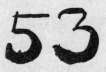

It feels like the house is trying to tear itself down even without Dad's help.

I run through the house to the very top windows overlooking the front yard. The floor rumbles. Windows shatter and bookshelves topple and lights flicker and burst as William tries to escape the nightmare world he had created.

I can tell from the intensity of the destruction that he's winning. We don't have much time. When he escapes, we're done for. All of us.

Come on, Dad, I think.

And then Dad and Mom are outside. Mom has

a few things stuffed into a backpack, as does Dad. I almost expect Mom to fight Dad—she never really believed in the ghost stuff—but maybe she believed more than she let on, because she doesn't seem to argue. He runs to the shed where I store my bike. She runs to the car. Is she driving off? Then she's back with some flattened cardboard boxes from the trunk.

Moments later, Dad is pouring gas on the wooden porch, and Mom is ripping the cardboard into strips before lighting them on fire and tossing them in the broken windows, setting her new curtains ablaze.

The fire catches immediately.

Spreads much faster than a fire should.

As if the house itself knows its existence as wrong.

Or as if, perhaps, the ghost children trapped here are somehow helping the blaze.

I watch as the fire eats away at the first floor, as Mom and Dad step back from the inferno.

Flames lick up to the windows, but I can't feel a thing as the hall behind me bursts into flame.

Another roar echoes through the house, but this time it isn't from William—it's from the fire that consumes the mansion that never should have existed.

Three shapes appear beside me.

Alice, who takes my hand.

And Max and Lela, who stand off to the side, staring out the window as the flames reach higher.

None of us speaks.

The house trembles and roars with flames and William's fury.

And as I squeeze Alice's hand, hoping against hope this will work, the house begins to cave in on itself. Brilliant light flares around us, from flames or something else. I close my eyes.

I picture my parents. I picture my friends.

The house collapses.

Epilogue

We stand outside the graveyard, Max and Lela and me.
The tombstones have all been propped upright, the
graves all put back in their rightful place. Two weeks
have passed since the house burned down and Max and
Lela and I reappeared here, at the graveyard, a little dusty
and a little shocked, but otherwise completely fine.

"It's sort of peaceful, you know?" Max says.

I nod.

"Yeah," I say. "But I'm glad it's not our time yet."

Lela nods stoically.

"You still don't remember anything?" I ask the
two of them.

They both shake their heads.

"It's like an old dream," Lela says. "Sometimes I can remember bits and pieces. But mostly I just remember being in your house and feeling like I was sleepwalking."

"Same," Max says.

They may not remember being ghosts, but I remember every moment. I'll never forget. That's a promise I've made to myself, and to Alice's memory.

She didn't reappear with us; a few of the other recently disappeared kids did. I haven't seen her ghost. I hope she finally found her mother and younger brother and could be truly happy. I look up to her statue, surrounded by the restored graves of everyone she wanted to be friends with.

Even though only my dad and Max and Lela believe me, I'll keep telling Alice's story. I'll keep telling the truth.

Lela and Max squeeze my hands, and then we turn and make our way from the restored graveyard down a beautiful stone path that we—and the rest of the town—helped build. I almost expected there to be some sort of uproar, but it was like the moment the house burned down, the town's attitude toward us changed. We were accepted. Maybe that was also part of the curse—so long as the house stood, whoever lived there was doomed to be an outsider.

Through the trees, and farther on, the ruins of my old house lie like broken bones on the side of the hill.

Now the only thing left standing of the old manor is a few pillars and some piles of brick.

"Do you guys want to have a sleepover at my place?" I ask.

"Now that it's not haunted?" Max asks. "Sure!"

That's the other nice thing; the townsfolk helped us find a new house pretty quickly, and Dad managed to get all his money back from the manor. Our new place is right in the center, where we can walk to everything. Finally, it feels like we're a part of the community.

"Does your dad still have all his equipment?" Lela asks. "I was thinking I could borrow it. Check out some other graveyards in town."

"No," I say with a chuckle. "He lost all of it. And I don't think he plans on replacing it."

I kind of expected Dad to ask a lot of questions after I came back. But he didn't. I think the entire episode cured him of wanting to experience the other side. We'd already had enough scares for a lifetime.

As we walk down the hill and into town, we pass by a group of kids I'd seen from school. They seem about our age, and they're heading up to the ruins.

"Where are you guys going?" Lela asks them, bold as ever.

The kids look at each other. The tallest one answers.

"We wanted to check it out," he says. "We heard it was haunted."

"It was," I say. "But it's not anymore."

The other kids shrug and keep on walking. Lela rolls her eyes and keeps going down the hill. I follow her, even though a part of me feels I should stop them. A part of me feels responsible. But the house is gone, and the haunting has passed. It's over. We're safe.

But as I go, I distinctly hear one of the kids behind us whisper.

"That's easy for them to say! But I've heard voices of some of the kids who passed on. They told me to come up here. They said they wanted to play a game . . ."

About the Author

K. R. Alexander is the pseudonym for author Alex R. Kahler.

As K. R., he writes creepy middle grade books for brave young readers. As Alex—his actual first name—he writes fantasy novels for adults and teens. In both cases, he loves writing fiction drawn from true life experiences. (But this book can't be real . . . can it?)

Alex has traveled the world collecting strange and fascinating tales, from the misty moors of Scotland to the humid jungles of Hawaii. He is always on the move, as he believes there is much more to life than what meets the eye.

You can learn more about his travels and books, including *The Collector, The Fear Zone,* and the books in the Scare Me series, on his website cursedlibrary.com.

He looks forward to scaring you again . . . soon.

Keep Reading For
More Scares From
K. R. Alexander

For the longest time, I thought I'd do anything to hear Isabella's voice again.

I would cut off all my hair and donate it to charity. I'd mow every lawn in the neighborhood, I'd get straight As on every test and piece of homework, I'd even eat all my vegetables at every meal.

Anything.

All I wanted was to hear her laugh again as we hid from our parents in our blanket fort, or have her braid my hair, or lie in our bedroom until way too late at night, talking about which teachers we thought were aliens or what we wanted to be when we grew up.

Isabella never got to grow up.

I thought I'd do anything to bring her back. To give her another chance at life. To have her be my sister again.

And then, with the help of my friends, we *did* bring her back . . .

. . . or at least we brought *something* back.

Be afraid.
Be very, very afraid...

Read more from

K. R. Alexander...

if you dare